She Gotta Be The Dopest To

Ride With The Coldest

Written By:

Kellz Kimberly & Kyoshi

Kyoshi's Acknowledgments

First and foremost I thank God for this gift, without Him none of this would be possible. He gave me a gift I never knew I had and I'm forever grateful for His continuous blessings in my life. I thank God for giving me the gift to reach other people, it's such an amazing feeling!

My pride and joy, my heartbeat, my everything, my reason for living Ky'Shawn Syncere, everything I do is for you. You are my motivation when times get tough and I wanna quit. I often say that you saved my life and that's a true statement, I truly thank God for you, I love you more than life itself.

To my guardian angel, my best friend, my big brother Antonio E. Williams. Not a second of any day goes by that you don't cross my mind, I miss you more than anyone will ever know. Until we meet again, continue to watch over me. I carry you in my heart every day and I love you very much. I feel your presence every day, so I know you riding with me! Continue to rest in peace my love.

Marquel, it's still hard to wrap my mind around the fact that you're really gone, every day is a struggle. I miss you so much big bro, shit don't even feel right without you here. Remembering our last conversation, you told me how proud of me you were and it felt good to hear that from you. I was proud of the man you were becoming and even though you're gone physically, I feel your presence every single day. I love you so freaking much man and I'll carry you in my heart forever. Sleep peacefully baby, fly high!

Dashawn, my little brother gone way too soon. Seeing DJ and not seeing you is just so freaking hard man. I've tried so hard to be strong, but losing you at such a young age hurts. We argued more than a little bit and you got on my nerves like any little brother would, but that was how we bonded. I didn't say it enough, but I loved you with everything in me and I miss you more than words can say. Fly high my baby and keep watch over your big sis!

My Kelly Kellz! What can I say about you? Lol! You are the absolute best! When I'm not feeling something I wrote, you're there to tell me I'm trippin (LOL)! Keep being you and letting that pen bang, cause you sick wit it! I'm super duper proud of the things you're doing, keep pushing! It was an honor to do this collab with you and you already know we bout to set the charts on fire with this one!

Ebony Smith my petty gang partner! I freaking LOVE you, you're the absolute best! Whenever I need someone to talk to I know that I can call you. The conversations we've had pushed me more than you know. It's a pleasure to know someone like you, you're such an amazing person!

Tiece Mickens, words can't express how grateful I am for you! Thank you for giving me a chance to be a part of your family. You're such an awesome person and I love me some you! I wanna be like you when I grow up! (lol) Nah but for real though, you are appreciated!

To my Miss Mickens/Tiece Presents/Tiece Mickens Presents family, thank you all for welcoming me with open arms! I look forward to working with you all! Let's keep settin the charts on fire!

To the ones that said I couldn't do it, I thank you. To the ones that gave up on me or turned their backs, I thank you. To the *one* boss that I ever had to fire me, I truly thank you, because that was the day I picked up a pen. Thirteen books later, I'm still standing, so I thank you!

There are so many more people to name, but that would take me all day! Just know that I appreciate you all and you each mean a lot to me. Thank you!

Follow me on Twitter @LilLadii0709

Facebook: Yoshi Chance or Author Kyoshi

Instagram: @she_certified27

Email me: chance.kyoshi@gmail.com

Kellz Kimberly Acknowledgements

I'm never really good at this type of thing so let me see if I can get this out quick and easy without any tears. I just honestly want to say thank you to all my readers and supporters. Y'all just don't know how much love I have for y'all. The reason I keep going with my writing is because of y'all. To every reader that has ever one clicked any of my books, left a review, shared a link I just want to say thank you from the bottom of my heart thank you.

Jamal you are my everything and what's understood doesn't have to be explained. Five years and counting, at the end of the day it will always be me and you.

I have to give a special shout out to Tiece. You are the real MVP for real, for real! You took a chance on me and I told you I got you, and I still do. I want to say thank you for everything you have done for me and continue to do. We may not see eye to eye on certain things, but you always show me you have my best interest at heart, and that means a lot. You are the true definition of a publisher. You have helped me in so many ways that it's crazy. It's not about the money with you and that's what I love. You genuinely want to see people succeed in this business. I have nothing but love for you and I will always have you for whatever.

Ebony my light skin, the relationship that we have built in the past year is one that I am grateful for. Our friendship goes beyond the literary world. You are honestly one of the most genuine people I have ever met and I just want to say thank you for just simple being there for me.

To everyone at Tiece Mickens Presents, y'all already know how we get down. The support we show each other is real and I'm glad to be signed with each and everyone of you.

Kyoshi what can I possibly say about you besides that you annoy me lol. Nah seriously though I appreciate the friendship that we have. We bug each other out but when we need each other we are right back to normal. Doing this collab with you has been long over due. You already know this link up was going to be real but now the readers know it too. Thank you for over looking my bipolar mood swings and working with me to write this banger. You already know what we about to do with this one shawty…

Niqua, the friendship that we have built in the last couple months is amazing. Whenever I write anything, you are one of the people I think to send it to first. I thank you for helping me and just reading everything I send you. Our friendship goes beyond the writing world and just know, we are turning up in Atlanta.

Victoria, you have been rocking with me since day one. I don't consider you a reader, I consider you a friend. You are always there to help when I get stuck or when I need you to read something. Plus, you are the voice of reason when I'm ready to do something crazy with these characters. You are another one of my favorite test readers because you tell me like it is instead of just saying you like it, and I appreciate that.

Rikida, you have been the biggest help when it came to this book. I don't know how many times I sent you this book so you could test read it for me, but every time I did send it, you gave great feedback. I don't think you know it, but you really pushed me with this book. Every time you gave me feedback, you were excited about the book, which pushed me to make the next chapters even better. Overall, I just want to say thank you.

Por'schea, girl, we clicked as soon as we started talking. I don't even view you as one of my readers, you're my friend. You are always there when I need you and I love that you are taking a chance on me. I got nothing but love for you and there is nothing else to do but go up from here.

To everyone in my group, BRP Presents: Bring Your Own Tea, thank you for rocking with me because y'all go hard for y'all girl. Its amazing how one group can bring so many women together who support and build each other up. I don't care what no one says my group is the shit.

To everyone that has helped me promote my book, read any of my books and given me feedback, I want to say thank you so much because it means a lot.

To all my readers that have Facebook, if y'all want to keep up with my new releases, sneak peeks and giveaways, join my Facebook group, BRP Presents: Bring Your Own Tea.

To get in contact with me, feel free to email me or hit me up on social media. Feel free to hit me up with questions and feedback.

Facebook: Kellz Kimberly

Facebook Group: BRP Presents: Bring Your Own Tea

Twitter: _KellzK

Instagram: __Lacedupchic

Snap Chat: kellzkayy

Email: Kellz@TMPresents.com

Chapter 1: Azuri

"Welcome to McDonalds, how can I help you?" I asked, without bothering to look up at the customer. I know I was supposed to because it was good customer service; I just couldn't find the energy.

"Yo, is your head too heavy to lift up or something? It's rude to talk to someone without looking them in the eyes, lil mama." At the sound of the voice, I snatched my head up with the quickness.

"I have been here for the past twelve hours; if I don't want to pick up my head to ask you what you want to eat, then guess what? I'm not going to do it. Now, would you like something to eat or not?" I was biting the corners of my mouth to keep from what I really wanted to say. I couldn't stand rude ass customers who thought they could talk to you any kind of way. This nigga picked the right one today.

"This bitch must not know how to treat a customer," the dude spat.

"Bitch! I'll show your little retarded looking ass who's the bitch," I sassed, ready to jump over the counter.

"Hey! Hey! What is going on over here?" the shift leader asked, trying to calm the situation down.

"I was trying to take their order when this little muthafucker started being rude and calling me bitches," I said.

"Man, fuck that bitch and this place," the same dude said again. There was another dude with him but he was just shaking his head. From the looks of it, ole boy was trying to hold in his laughter.

"I'm gonna have to ask you two to leave or I will not hesitate to call the cops," my shift leader said, making sure to grab the store phone.

"No need for all of that. Lil mama, I apologize for how my brother acted. Here's something for your troubles," the dude who

1

was just standing there said, pulling out a knot and handing me a hundred-dollar bill.

I looked at it like it was the plague. I picked it up, made sure to rip it in little pieces, and threw it in his face.

"I don't need nor do I want your money. You think you can fix your brother's foul ass mouth with a fucking hundred-dollar bill. My respect cost a hundred times that much," I told them. Both dudes stood there shocked before walking away. I half expected for the rude one to have something else to say, since he didn't know how to keep his mouth shut.

"Girl, you dumb for that. I would have kept that money." My shift leader giggled.

"Dude disrespected me and thinks he can fix the issue with money. It doesn't work that way with me."

"That shit would have worked on me without a doubt."

"That's why you and I are two different people. Honestly, I just want to go home; I'm not even feeling this right now." My feet were swollen and my body was beyond tired.

"You can go but make sure you leave that attitude at the door when you come in on your next shift," she scolded.

"Yea ok," I told her.

She popped out my drawer and I made a beeline for the office. I quickly counted out my drawer and bagged my money. Once everything was done, I dropped my money, grabbed all of my things, and was out the door.

It was springtime but because I lived in Coney Island, which was surrounded by water, there was still a chill in the night air. I pulled my small sweater as far down as I could and began walking the twenty blocks to my house. I hated walking on Mermaid late at night; niggas out here were always wildin' for respect. Bullets didn't have no names on them and they didn't give a fuck. Coney Island has been my home for the past twenty-one years; the fact I still get nervous walking down the street late at night should tell you something.

"Wassup Azuri!" I heard someone call out when I hit 25th street.

I slightly waved, then kept it pushing. No matter the time of day or night, you could always find someone hugging the block on two fifth. As you heard ole dude say, my name is Azuri Knox. Y'all probably thinking why is a twenty-one-year-old working at McDonald's, right? Well, this was the hand life dealt me. Growing up was rough; I was the stereotypical black girl from the hood. Single mother because pops didn't want to face his responsibilities; food stamps and government cheese was the norm for me. My mother worked as a home health aide. She didn't make much money, but she made enough to make sure that we had our necessities. There was no copping the latest Jordan's for me; all I knew was uptowns. I would be lucky if my mother could afford a pair twice a year.

Since my mother wasn't going to be able to get us out the hood, I decided to be the one to step up to the plate. All my life, I heard education was key, so I worked my ass off in high school. Instead of being in boys' faces, I had my face in a book. I tried my hardest when it came to school and I must say, I did alright. I got a couple partial scholarships but it wasn't enough. My senior year in high school is when I started working at McDonald's, trying to save up money. By the time I graduated, I had a little something something put away for my education. It wasn't much but at least it was something.

My dreams of going to college, then getting a high paying job and moving my mama out the hood, crashed and burned when I found out my mother had a mild case of Lupus. My mother's illness was random to me because it came out of nowhere. First, it started with the headaches, then her muscles aching and, from there, it went to weight loss. I made her go to the hospital, once I saw the rash on her cheeks and the bridge of her nose. The doctor told us the exact cause of Lupus is unknown; some say people are born with certain genes that effect how the immune system works and then there are triggers. To say my hopes and dreams were shattered would be an insult to how I really felt. My mother was my best friend and I loved her to death; she was always there when I needed her, so I was going to be there when she needed me.

With my mother being in and out of the doctors and having so many restrictions on what she can and couldn't do, I decided that it would be best for her just not to work. She fought me about it at first, but once I explained to her that I would rather work my ass off then to bury my mother, she got the hint. I worked as hard as I did for her to make sure she was as comfortable as she could be. Losing my mother wasn't an option for me. I would rather sacrifice my needs and wants before seeing her go.

As I walked up to my building in Gravesend Projects, I heard someone call out to me. I wasn't going to turn around but the person was persistent.

"My name ain't aye and what do you want?" I sassed. I heard a light chuckle and watched as the figure jogged towards me. When the person got closer, I recognized him as the rude ass from my job.

Chapter 2: Gotti

"Aye, you can chill with all that muthafuckin sass; a nigga came over here to apologize to yo simple ass for calling you a bitch earlier!" I snapped.

"I didn't ask you to apologize to me nigga and furthermore, I don't want or need yo fuckin apology!" she snapped back, rolling her neck and shit.

I studied her ass and had to admit that lil mama was fine as fuck, but I wouldn't let her simple ass know that. She was mocha colored, with pouty lips and a body that wouldn't quit. If she knew how to act, then I might let her see what it was like to fuck wit a boss.

"Well, fuck you too then wit yo busted ass! A nigga can't even be nice to a bitch and apologize without all the extra shit. Fuck outta here ma, you got the wrong nigga cause I ain't the one. Now, go in there and wash yo ass, out here smelling like overcooked oil, fries, and burnt burgers, and shit," I spat before turning to walk away.

"Fuck you too, bitch made nigga!" she spat.

I bit the inside of my jaw cause I was two point five seconds away from spazzing on her ass. Instead, I took the mature way out and kept walking cause lil mama really ain't know who the fuck I was.

"I told yo ass to leave that girl alone," my brother said through his laughter as I climbed in the driver's side.

"Fuck that bitch, man, wit her stuck up bad attitude havin ass. How the fuck you stuck up, but you work at Mickey D's; how does that shit even work?" I asked seriously.

Lil mama had got under my skin and I couldn't figure out why. A nigga like me ain't never went out of my way to apologize to a bitch, ever.

Some of y'all might think I'm an asshole and you're absolutely right, but I give zero fucks about what the next muthafucka think about me. I'm twenty-five-year-old Kashmir Banks, but to the streets, I'm Gotti, the fuckin king of New York. Born and raised in the boogie down Bronx; shit, a nigga had to get it how I lived.

I ain't have no sad ass story about my moms being on dope and my pops leaving. They were very much still together after twenty-seven years. Shit, my dukes was a fuckin rider; she had been through hell and back wit my pops, but she stayed by his side.

Pops was a OG in my hood, so it was only right that when he stepped down, me and my brother stepped up. Don't get shit twisted though, we had to work for our shit; it wasn't just handed to us.

I was the realest nigga that NY had ever seen and even though I was an asshole most of the time, I was a good nigga; I just wasn't beat for no bullshit. My ringing phone snapped me out of my thoughts.

"Speak!"

"Hey Gotti daddy, I miss you!" Zena purred into the phone.

"Aye, what the fuck I tell you about that daddy shit! You ain't come from neither one of my fuckin nutsacks, now what the fuck you want, Z?"

"Damn Gotti, do you always got to be so fuckin rude?"

"This shit ain't nothin new to yo big faced ass; now, tell me what the fuck you want or get the fuck off my line!"

I knew I was spazzing on Zena for no reason, but I was still tight about that shit wit lil mama. It was probably mean for me to take it out on Zena, but she knew how I got down. So, she knew more than anybody how much I hated my time being wasted.

"Ummm... I..."

"Fuck off my line man!" I spat before hanging up on her.

"Damn nigga, yo ass need some fuckin pussy or something, snapping and shit like yo period on!" my little brother Jahzir said with his face balled up.

"Fuck outta here nigga, I get more pussy than yo bitch ass," I replied, smirking.

"Nigga, what the fuck ever!" He laughed.

"But, on some real shit Gotti, you spazzed on ol girl for no fuckin reason at all. She was only tryin to take your order and shit, but you called her a bitch; that shit won't cool," he said seriously.

I didn't respond, mainly because I didn't give a fuck, but a part of me knew that he was right. But shit, I tried to apologize and she gave me her ass to kiss, so fuck her.

"Man, fuck all that shit you talkin bout, what them traps lookin like?" I asked him.

"Everything straight, money flowin, same ol shit." He shrugged.

I nodded my head and turned up the music, letting Jim Jones bump through the radio. My mind drifted back to lil mama from McDonald's. I don't know what it was about her little ass, but lil mama was tough.

Her fuckin mouth was hell though; I was gon have to tame that shit. I made it up in my mind that I was gon have her lil ass though and you could believe that shit.

After dropping Jahzir off at his crib, I drove around the city wit her little ass on my mind heavy. I didn't know what the fuck it was about her, but I couldn't shake her little ass and that was rare for me. I fucked these bitches and never gave them a second thought, that's just how I rolled.

I didn't give these hoes false dreams or high hopes of shit; I told them exactly what it was from the jump. Instead of going home, I headed to Zena's house. Pulling up, I parked my whip and hopped out.

I didn't even bother knocking, I had a key, so I walked right in.

"Gotti, what you doing here?" she asked as soon as I walked in.

"I gotta have a reason to come by this muthafucka now?"

"No baby, that's not what I meant; I'm just surprised, that's all," she replied, softening her tone.

"Fuck all that shit you talkin, come over here and rock the mic," I spat before sitting down.

Without another word, she got down on her knees and did as she was told. I shook my head and got comfortable, but once again, lil mama crossed my mind. It went from Zena rocking the mic to her sexy chocolate ass and a nigga dick got harder.

I didn't know what the fuck was up with me, but one thing I did know was that I was gon see lil mama soon and whether she liked it or not, she was gon be the first lady of the streets.

Chapter 3: Azuri

The next morning, I woke up still pissed at ole boy. If it's one thing I couldn't stand, it was a disrespectful, rude ass nigga. How he call himself apologizing but still ended up calling me a bitch? The nigga had me six thirty hot. Hopefully, last night would be the last time I saw his ass because the next time I saw him, the nigga was gonna get read.

I rolled out of bed and made my way to the bathroom. Using the bathroom, washing my face, and brushing my teeth was part of my morning routine. Hygiene was very important to me, which was why dude pissed me off even more. Talking about I smelled like overcooked oil, fries, and burnt burgers. Tuh, bish where is what I should've said. I smelt like strawberries and vanilla at all times.

"Azuri!" I heard my mother call out.

I walked out of the bathroom and into the kitchen where the aroma of eggs, bacon, and pancakes lingered.

"Ma, why are you yelling? I was only in the bathroom." I sat at the table while my mother prepared the plates. Having breakfast together was something we did every morning. I guess you could call it a tradition. No matter what time I had to go into work, my mother would always get up two hours earlier, so we could chat over breakfast. She even did it when I was in school.

"I forgot to find out what time you worked today. I didn't know if you were here or not."

"I did a double yesterday, so I'm off today," I told her, digging into my food.

"I wish you would take more than one day off sweetie. I'm not as sick as I used to be. I can always go back to work."

"No, Nala, you are not working and that's that. You sell plates, isn't that good enough? I don't need you out here working your ass off and getting sicker than you already are." The only time I called my mother by her first name was when I was serious about something.

"Azuri, I'm so sick of you calling me by my first name like I'm the child," she sassed. "Selling plates is just something I do with your aunt, so I'm not bored in the house all the time. You are only young once baby. I don't want you wasting your life away at a dead end job."

"I'm not wasting my life away. I'm doing what needs to be done to ensure that you stay healthy and we have a place to stay. Going out and clubbing isn't me ma, so I'm not even missing out on anything."

This wasn't the first time we had this conversation and I'm sure it wasn't going to be the last. She always wanted to bring up how much I was letting life pass me by. I would rather have her in my life then to live my life to fullest. No matter how many times I told her that, it was like she didn't get it. It was either that or she refused to understand.

"Azuri, I love you and I love the fact that you care enough about me to put your own life on hold, but it's not necessary. The doctor told me that I have been doing better and that it's okay for me to get out more." I raised my eyebrow because I didn't believe anything she had just said.

"Then tell the doctor to write me a note telling me exactly what you just said."

"I am forty years old and I'm not going to answer to my twenty-one-year-old daughter."

"If you say so." I shrugged. I got up, grabbing both of our plates and brought them to the sink. I quickly cleaned them, then headed back towards my room. I didn't have to work today, so I was going to get in a couple more hours of sleep. Just as I was laying down, I heard a faint knock at my door.

"Come in."

"Azuri, I just want you to stop treating me as if I'm on my death bed," my mother said, peeking into the room.

"I don't treat you as if you're on your death bed. I treat as if I'm trying to keep you away from your death bed. I will come with you to your next doctor's appointment and if the doctor gives you the green light to go back to work, then I will be okay with it."

"I'll take that deal. I'm going over to your aunt's house. Don't stay sleep all day get out and get some fresh air."

"Okay ma, love you."

"I love you too, baby."

She closed the door and a single tear slipped from my eye. My mother was my world and to think about losing her would kill me. However, I couldn't keep her locked up either. The same way she wanted me to live my life, I had to let her live hers.

* * * *

My phone vibrating woke me out of my peaceful slumber. I grabbed it and looked at the name displayed on the screen. My eyes were barely open, but I managed to still roll them. It was my cousin Naomi calling. Naomi was my aunt Violet's daughter. She was two years older than me, but you wouldn't be able to tell from the way she acted. We were close but she irked my nerves. She was the definition of a project chick; she wore the title proudly too.

"Naomi, what do you want?"

"Maybe you need to go back to sleep then wake up again because you obviously woke up on the wrong side of the bed."

"You have two seconds to tell me what you want, Naomi. I'm tired as hell and this is my only day off."

"I was just calling to see if you wanted to go to Rucker Park with me."

"What's going on out there?" Rucker Park wasn't somewhere I frequented often; them Harlem niggas were known to start shooting without warning.

"Some niggas from the Bronx are going against some Harlem niggas."

"How do you even know that when you live all the way in Brooklyn? Wait, why niggas playing basketball outside in the middle of April? It's not even that nice out." I don't even know why I asked because Naomi was nosey as hell. She knew people's business before they even knew it.

"You already know I stay up on everything. Stop asking so many questions; I'm starting to think you the feds." She giggled. "Get dressed; I'll come pick you up in thirty."

"You irk my soul Naomi."

"Yeah, I love you too, cousin." She hung up the phone and I threw my cell towards the end of my bed.

I had no plans on leaving out the house today. Whenever I was off, I liked to just lounge around the house. After thinking if I really wanted to go, I picked up my phone to call Naomi back and tell her I wasn't going. I went to hit the call button and my mother's words echoed in my head. *You're only young once.* I decided to suck it up and go have some fun for once.

Even though I showered last night, I still jumped in to take a quick one. Getting out, I lotioned my body with Bourbon Strawberry and Vanilla body cream from Bath and Body. I threw on a pair of ripped up black jeans with a red Nike hoodie. On my feet, I wore my flu game 12's and not the retro shits either. I was a true sneaker head in every sense of the word. I usually wore my hair in a ponytail but, for some reason, I wanted to do something different. I parted it down the middle and let it hang freely. My hair stopped at the middle of my back; it was thick and too much to handle most days, which was why I wore it in a ponytail.

I gave myself the once over before running out the door. I said hey to a couple of the dudes I knew that were outside my building, then jumped in Naomi's 2014 Honda Accord.

"It's about time you came outside for a minute. I thought your ass was going to stay in the damn house."

"I'm sure if I tried, you would have come upstairs and forced me out."

"You damn right." She laughed.

I busied myself on my phone the whole entire ride. I made sure to text my mother, letting her know where I was. When she texted me back, she was a little too happy that I was out the house. Pulling up to the park, the shit was packed. The shit looked like a car show. There was everything from Escalades to Mustang from cheap hoopties to luxury cars. Niggas weren't here for a basketball game; they came out here to floss.

"Please don't embarrass me out here," Naomi said, getting out the car

"Don't you think I should be telling you that?" I snapped. "You out here dressed like it's ninety degrees. Too Short isn't around looking for hoes for his music video." I kid you not. Naomi had on a tight ass black dress that stopped before it started, not to mention the six inch pumps she had on.

"Don't hate, appreciate. You see all these niggas out here, I'm ready to make one of them daddy. Shit, they might be the reason the show started but I plan on stopping this shit."

"Naomi, all attention isn't good attention," I reminded her.

"Shit if it ain't. Good or bad, these niggas and bitches still looking."

"Whatever," I said, ending the conversation. It made no sense to go back and forth with her ass because she wasn't going to learn.

Naomi ended up going in a different direction from the court. Instead of following her, I went to go find a seat. Naomi didn't know shit about basketball, but it was my favorite sport. I played since middle school but stopped my senior year. I was about to step foot on the court with my face all in my phone when I walked into somebody's chest.

"I may be little but I'm not a fucking ant; I know your big ass saw me coming," I spat, as I dusted myself off and got up.

"How many times I have to tell your fucking hard headed ass about looking muthafuckers in the face." I looked up, already knowing who the familiar voice belonged to.

"Nigga, I can look wherever the fuck I want. You don't own my fucking eyes," I spat. "Matter of fact, what are you even doing talking to me? Nigga, be gone." I waved his ass off and went to sit down before the game started.

While sitting there, I felt someone burning a whole into the side of my face. I looked up and it was the same nigga. I chucked up my middle finger and rolled my eyes at his ass, then looked back at my phone. I began shaking my leg because I was all the way pissed off. I wished my ass would've stayed home because now I would have to deal with this stupid ass nigga.

Chapter 4: Gotti

This was the second time her funny looking ass had come out her mouth wrong to me, but if I had any say so, it would definitely be her last. I chuckled slightly when she shot me the finger, cause I could tell I got under her skin.

Me and my niggas were out here at Rucker; I had some money on my lil niggas from the Bronx and they were doing these Harlem cats dirty out here. Ever so often, my eyes drifted over to where lil mama sat and I smirked when I caught her eyeing me a few times.

Bitches were feenin for my attention, but my focus was on her and I couldn't tell you why. Maybe it was because she dissed a nigga more than once and I was used to bitches falling all over me, like the one that was currently in my grill now.

I knew all about Naomi and her reputation was one of the worst. It was a damn shame too, cause shorty was cute, but I couldn't do nothing for her.

"Hey Gotti, when you gon put a real bitch on your team?" she asked flirtatiously.

"Whenever the fuck I see one," I spat.

"You a rude ass nigga," she snapped.

"And you a hoe ass bitch, so what's your point?" I asked, before iggin her simple ass.

She looked like she wanted to say something, but one look from me shut all that shit the fuck down. Naomi knew how I got down and she also knew that I would embarrass the fuck outta her ass out here. Bitch out here in a fuckin mini dress and stilettos at the fuckin court, fuck they do that at?

"Damn Gotti, you hell on these hoes," my nigga Quest laughed.

"Like Snoop said, I don't love these hoes," I joked.

Once again, my eyes drifted over to lil mean ass and I eyed her from head to toe, smirking lightly when I saw she was matching my fly. I loved a bitch that could be fly dressed up or dressed down and fully clothed; she was killing all these hoes out here.

"Aye Gotti, you tryin to run this next game?" Quest asked me, as the previous game came to an end.

"Nah, I'm just a spectator homie," I replied.

"Don't tell me you scared to get that ass whooped," Dru joked.

"Yea aight, you don't even believe that shit." I laughed.

I was starting forward all four years of high school; shit, a nigga could've even went pro, but the streets were calling a nigga. After hearing these niggas talk shit, I decided to go ahead and put on a show for the future first lady.

Pulling off my hoodie and chain, I made my way over to where lil mama was sitting. I tossed my phone in her lap, slid my chain over her head, and laid my hoodie beside her.

"Keep an eye on that shit for me, while I school these niggas right quick," I told her.

"Nigga please, who the fuck do I look like?" she asked angrily.

"Like my future." I winked at her, causing her mean ass to blush.

"I'm not-"

"Look here lil mama, you bout the only muthafucka I would trust to hold my shit and that's a good thing. So, hold onto that shit for ya nigga and maybe I'll take yo mean ass to Coney Island or some shit."

"You're an arrogant bastard," she said, sucking her teeth.

"You like that shit though, I can see it in your eyes," I replied.

Boldly bending down, I grabbed her chin and looked into her eyes. She tried to pull away, which only made me grab it tighter.

"Don't play wit me, ma; I will fuckin embarrass yo simple ass out here. Now, don't let nothin happen to my shit or we gon have some fuckin problems." I winked before kissing her lips and walking away, just as my phone rang.

"Your phone!" she called after me.

"Answer that shit or ignore it!" I called over my shoulder.

My niggas were looking at me in disbelief, but my brother just grinned and shook his head; he knew what was up. Bitches looked at lil mama wit envy, but I dared they asses to say anything to her. We ran two games of twenty-one and a nigga was tired as fuck, but five grand richer, so I wasn't complaining.

"We still headin out tonight?" Quest asked me.

"I don't even know, a nigga just really tryna chill," I replied, glancing at lil mama.

She had her face buried in her phone, but lifted her head when she felt eyes on her. I blew her a kiss and she rolled her eyes before putting her head back down. That was another thing I was gon have to fix; when fuckin wit a boss, you keep your head up at all times.

"Aight, just get wit me later and let me know," he said and I nodded before slapping him up.

Coolly making my way over to lil mama, I snatched her up and sat down with her on my lap.

"You see yo nigga out there handlin shit?" I asked, burying my face in her neck.

"Umm, nigga, if you don't let me the fuck go, we gon have some problems!" she snapped, trying to get up, but I held her tighter.

"Aye, chill the fuck out wit that shit, ma," I said, slapping her thigh hard as hell.

She bit down on her bottom lip and closed her eyes, while I looked on amused. Her little ass was so mad; she was trembling.

"Azuri, you ready to go?" Naomi hating ass asked walking up.

"Nah, she ain't ready to go," I replied.

"I was talking to my cousin," she spat with her hands on her hips.

"But bitch, I was talking to you! I said she ain't ready to go and when she is, I'll take her the fuck home. Now, go find a dick to put in your mouth and leave us the fuck alone, damn!" I snapped.

Lil mama looked at me with wide eyes and popped the back of my head, causing me to grab her wrist.

"Watch that shit," I warned.

"Tell yo apple head ass cousin that you good, so she can get the fuck out my presence; I'm sick of lookin at her hoe ass."

"Gotti, you don't got to be a fuckin asshole!"

"Evidently that's the only got damn language rats understand, move the fuck around wit that shit Naomi," I spat before biting the inside of my jaw.

"I'm good Naomi, I'll call you when I get home," Lil mama finally spoke up.

"You sure?"

"Yea, she fuckin sure, you act like I'm tryin to hurt her or some shit! When she wit me, she always gon be good; now, get the fuck on."

She rolled her eyes, told lil mama to call her, and walked off fuming. That shit was comical to me cause she would still be trying to fuck a nigga after this shit.

"You ain't got to be so fuckin mean," Lil mama spat.

"Sometimes, mean is the only shit people understand." I shrugged, standing her up.

Pulling my hoodie on, she handed me my phone and I slipped it in my pocket without even checking it. She tried to take off my chain, but I deaded that shit.

"Keep that on, I like the way it look on you." I winked before grabbing her hand.

"Where are we going?" she asked, as I started my Mustang.

"Does it matter," I replied.

"Yes, it does, nigga; I don't know you," she sassed.

"I'm Kashmir," I told her, holding out my hand.

She looked at me, before a small grin broke out on her face.

"Azuri," she said, shaking my hand.

"Well Ms. Azuri, you tryin to fuck wit a nigga for a lil while?" I asked her.

I could tell she was a little hesitant, but I wasn't trying to fuck or no shit, well not yet anyway. On some real shit, I just wanted to chill wit her pretty ass and get to know her.

"Just for a little while," she finally replied.

I nodded my head and pulled out of the parking lot with her riding shotgun. This shit was weird as fuck. No bitch had ever rode in my shit, not unless my dick was down they throat. But here I was, driving through the city, stealing glances at her ass every so often. Lil mama had my head fucked up and what she failed to realize was that she was already mine, in every sense of the word.

Chapter 5: Azuri

The whole car ride, I had my face in my phone. One would think I was talking to everyone in the world but, in reality, I was trying to calm my nerves. I couldn't stand his rude ass but at the same time, he did something to me. From the stares I was getting from the chicks, I knew he had to be of someone of importance.

"Get out the car and leave the phone in the seat. I'm the only nigga you should be talkin to right now."

"I guess we back to the asshole again." I placed my phone in the cup holder, then proceed out the car. Instead of waiting for him, I walked over to the boardwalk, getting close enough to see the view of the ocean. This was one of the things I loved about living in Coney Island. Looking out to the sea was always so calm and relaxing for me. I didn't get to come up here often because of work but when I did, I made the best of it.

"Azuri, the fuck you walk off like that for?" Kashmir walked up behind me, wrapping his arms around my waist. I tried to break the embrace but he had the death grip on me.

"What was I supposed to do, stand there and let you disrespect me?" I quizzed.

"Nobody was disrespecting you, ma. All I said was to leave you phone in the car. A nigga couldn't even talk to yo ass on the drive up here."

"It's not about what you said, it's how you said it."

"What fuckin' difference does it make? Either way I would have said it, you still would've had the same fucked up attitude."

"Oh shit, *I'm* the one with the fucked up attitude?" I asked, playing as if I was shocked.

"Azuri, don't even do that. Every time I come into contact with yo ass, you running off at the mouth. Got me out here thinkin bout getting you a got damn muzzle."

"Nigga, did you just call me a fucking dog? Kashmir, get the fuck off me and leave me the fuck alone. I don't even know why I came out here with yo stupid ass."

This time, when I tried to break out of the hold he had on me, I was successful. I glared at him before walking further down the boardwalk. I lived blocks away so walking home was nothing to me.

"Azuri, hold up!" I heard him call after me.

I sped up walking because I no longer had anything to say to his ass. It was like, whenever I saw this nigga, he disrespected me. The girls he usually fucked with must have been okay with him talking to them; however, he wanted but that shit wasn't going to fly with me.

"Yo, I said hol' the fuck up damn!" He grabbed my arm and I yanked it away from him.

"Don't you fucking put yo' hands on me," I spat.

"Chill out with all that fly shit coming out yo' mouth."

"Why do I have to be the one to chill out when you started this shit? Talking about you're going to buy me a muzzle. Is that how your mother raised you to talk to woman? Does yo' big headed ass know nothing about respect?"

"Iight, I hear what you're saying but don't ever speak that ill shit about my moms."

"Out of everything I said, the only thing your ass paid attention to was me saying something about your mom?" I laughed a little because he couldn't be serious. "Later Kashmir." I hit him with the deuces sign and continued walking. I didn't get very far because this nigga swooped me up in his arms like I was a fucking rag doll.

"Put me the fuck down." I kicked and hit him, but he didn't seem fazed by it.

"Shut yo' little ass up, iight." He walked over to a bench and sat me on his lap.

I folded my arms across my chest and pouted, as if I was five. I knew I looked childish; shit, I didn't care though.

"Iight Azuri, you're right. I shouldn't have talked to you that way." I looked at him through squinted eyes.

"You can keep that weak ass apology because I don't want nor need it. All I need is my phone out your car, so I can go home." When I first walked off, I forgot all about my phone. Now that I remembered it, I wasn't going nowhere without it.

"Is your phone your life or something? Fuck that piece of shit; you with me now, so chill the fuck out. You gonna make me fuck yo little ass up behind a fucking phone."

"How do you apologize, then go off again in the next breath?"

"Ma, I don't, but I'm not even trying to talk about that. I'm just trying to get to know you, not even on no sexual tip either. I want to know the real you because the snappy munchkin I got sitting on my lap right now isn't even you."

I blushed at what he said and quickly looked towards the ground. I fiddled my thumbs around, hoping to avoid what he just said.

"Azuri, I'm tired of you looking down and shit. Do you have low self-esteem or some shit?"

My head quickly shot up, ready to go off, but he cut me off.

"I'm not even trying to offend you or nothing."

"No, I don't have low self-esteem."

"Then look a nigga in the eye when you're in the presence of a boss."

For the first time since we met, I looked deep into his eyes. They were a pretty hue of brown with a hint of green. I felt myself getting lost in them.

"Iight, now you looking too deep in my eyes now." He laughed, mushing my head to the side.

"You make me sick." I giggled. I could help but to laugh too; his laughter was infectious.

"Oh shit, she smiles and what a beautiful smile it is." Once again, my ass was blushing and looking down at the ground. He cupped my chin, lifting my head back up.

"When I make you blush or give you butterflies, don't turn your head away from me. Show me how I make you feel. Let a nigga know that he on his job when it comes to you." Kashmir wasn't yelling, but he had so much authority in his voice. All I could do was nod my head because my voice was stuck in my throat.

"If you can't handle me making you smile, how you supposed to handle me making them panties wet." As quickly as my voice left, it came back.

"Nigga please, in your dreams. The day you get my juices flowin will be the day pigs fly. You kind of slow and shit, so let me put it in layman terms. Never gonna get it, never gonna get it," I sang.

"Don't quit that dusty ass job at McDonald's because singing ain't yo thang. You almost fucked up my ears with that screeching you was just doin."

"Whatever." I rolled my eyes at him because he was always playing.

"On the real, why you working at McDonald's? I'm not judging you or nothing; a nigga just want to know."

"I need money and it pays the bills." I kept it short, sweet, and simple.

"You never wanted to go to school or nothing? Just from looking at you, I can tell you're a smart girl with a good head on yo shoulders."

"Of course I wanted to go to school but life got in the way. During my senior year of high school, my mom was diagnosed with a mild case of Lupus. She had to stop working and I had to start. My mom's health is the most important thing to me."

"I can feel you on that one," he said. "But yo, if you're Naomi's cousin, how come I never seen yo ass around? Naomi be fucking everywhere, that bitch is like a roach."

"Don't talk about my cousin like that." I tried to stifle my laugh because that shit was funny. Naomi was always somewhere doing something.

"You know you want to laugh ma; don't hold that shit in. Her ass be in everyone mix and her reputation ain't too pretty."

"I don't chill with my cousin like that because I'm always at work." I shrugged. I knew about Naomi's reputation, but I didn't judge; she was grown.

"I got me a hard working girl," he boasted

"You don't have a damn thing. I'm not your girl," I sassed.

"Yeah, that's what your mouth say. Tell me more about you, Azuri." His voice softened and his eyes lingered over my body. I wasn't uncomfortable by his gaze; I was, in fact, turned on a little.

"There isn't much to tell. I'm twenty-one, my birthday is in July, team Leo. In this crazy thing we call life, all I have is my Aunt Violet, who is Naomi's mom, Naomi, and my mother. I live a rather simple life. Tell me something about you."

"I'm twenty-five and a boss, enough said."

"You are so annoying, I swear."

"If that's what you want to call it. Keep talking about you, tho."

"Why do you want to know so much about me?" I have never had a dude take this much interest in me, especially one that was as rude as him.

"I already told you I want to know the real you. I want to know what it takes to earn the key to your heart. This isn't even game; I'm giving you that real shit ma."

Once again, he had my ass blushing and shit. I wish I was able to control it; I didn't want him to know he had this effect over me. We stayed out on the boardwalk all the way til two in the morning. We would've stayed out there longer, but I needed to get some rest for work. He dropped me off and, before I got out the car, we exchanged numbers. He told he would hit me up sometime tomorrow. I just nodded my head because I wasn't going to get my hopes up. I was on the fence about him. I couldn't put my finger on it but it was as if Kashmir was two people in one. You had the rude and ignorant side of him, then you had the smooth talking loveable side. Getting in the house, I ate, showered, and got into bed, all the while thoughts of Kashmir were on my mind. This was the second night he was on my mind and I wasn't mad at it at all.

Chapter 6: Gotti

I had never sat and just talked to a chick, but I could do that shit all day long with Azuri. Just being in her presence had me captivated, had me wanting to be everything she needed and wanted. The shit she told me about her moms made me respect her much more than I already did. •

You wouldn't find too many bitches out here that were that selfless. My mom was my heart and I would do anything for her, so I could dig that shit. The whole ride to my crib, I thought of ways to not only help Azuri, but take some of the strain off her as well.

All this shit was new to my black ass, cause like I said, I fucked 'em and kept it pushing. But something told me that Azuri was gon be the one that broke my ass down. I fucked wit lil mama cause she didn't take my shit and she wasn't one for the disrespect. She didn't give a fuck who I was; she wasn't afraid to buck back at my ass.

I knew she was doing all she could to help her mother, but I also knew that she had goals and ambitions that she wanted to achieve. If I didn't do shit else, I was damn sure gon make sure she reached every single goal.

A nigga was dog ass tired, so once I got home, I showered and took my ass straight to bed.

* * * *

I pulled up to my parents' crib out in Long Island; it had been a few days since I had seen them and I already knew my moms was bout to go in on my ass.

"Well, well, well, the prodigal son has returned." She smiled as I walked into the sitting room.

"Chill out ma, it's only been a few days," I chuckled, kissing her cheek.

Taking a seat beside her, she rubbed my head and put her arm around me. In the streets, I was the infamous Gotti. But, to Gina Banks, I was just Kashmir or Kashy, as she called me.

"What's been goin on son?" she asked me.

"Same ol same ol ma, you know how I do." I shrugged.

"Mmm hmm, I sure do know how you do. When you gon settle down boy? Hell, I want some grandbabies."

I groaned inwardly; this was always the topic of our conversation.

"Chill ma, I got all the time in the world to have kids," I told her.

"Well, I don't want you to have no babies when I'm old and gray; I want to enjoy them while I'm young and fine," she snapped, causing me to laugh.

At forty-seven, she didn't look a day over thirty. Her rich dark skin, bright almond eyes, and slim physique had her putting a lot of these young bitches out here to shame.

"You always say that ma." I grinned.

"Cause it's the truth, shit! Just make sure when you do have one, it ain't by one of these nasty bitches out here that follow yo ass around like a little puppy."

"I think I found her ma," I blurted out.

Moms was gon give it to me straight with no chaser, so I decided to tell her about Azuri from the jump.

"Well, don't keep me in suspense, tell me about her," she said, sitting up grinning widely.

I ran down the whole story, from the first time I met Azuri up until I dropped her off last night.

"First things first," she said, before she slapped me upside my head.

"Owww ma, what you do that for?" I frowned, rubbing my head.

"I should've hit yo rude ass harder than that! You know I raised you to respect women, well, except for the ones that don't respect themselves, but you were wrong Kashy and if I was her, I wouldn't have no words for yo ass," she spat angrily.

"She ain't got no choice." I shrugged.

"The hell you say! She does have a choice and if she don't want to deal with you, then you can't force her. Now, it's obvious that this girl is a different breed and she don't put up with no shit, which is exactly what you need. Don't try to force that girl into something; be her friend first because from the sounds of it, that's what she needs."

"I can't explain it ma, just being around her makes me want to be better. She ain't impressed wit my street cred; she could care less and that makes me want her even more. Not only that, but I respect her for putting her dreams on hold to take care of her mother. I just want to help her be whatever she wants to be and achieve whatever she wants to achieve," I told her honestly.

"I understand that Kashy, but if you go tossing your money around, you gon make her feel like a charity case and that's the last thing she needs. Be her friend, be there when she needs you the most, and most of all respect her. A woman, a *real* woman, don't give a damn about what you have; all she wants is you. I like her already because she don't take your shit and she ain't afraid to check yo black ass."

I took in everything she said and she was right. I never wanted Azuri to feel like I looked at her with pity because I didn't; I admired her. Me disrespecting her was wrong on all levels, but her fuckin mouth was hell. Azuri knew how to get under my skin because she didn't back down to me and I wasn't used to that shit.

"How about you do something nice for her, something that's out of your comfort zone? Help her escape, if only for a little while; I guarantee she'll appreciate that," she suggested.

"You just make sure that you're really into this girl and you're not just infatuated with her. I know you, Kashmir, and I know you throw women away like they goin out of style. If you not serious about her, then leave her be because all you're gonna do is break her heart. Just be her friend baby," she told me.

"I'm past the point of infatuation ma; Azuri is just different and that's what I like about her. The damn girl works at McDonald's at twenty-one; it might not be the best job, but I love the fact that shorty get her own."

"Any woman that can't go out here and get her own is a waste of space. Shit, your daddy was the king of the streets and I taught fifth grade the whole time. Even though your daddy didn't want me to work, it just wasn't in me to sit my ass in the house. It sounds like you got a winner on your hands, just make sure you don't fuck it up."

I chuckled lightly. Mom dukes was gangsta and soft at the same damn time, but I loved her crazy ass. For the next two hours, I just kicked it with her, until my pops came in and told me to get the fuck out.

Riding through the streets, I started to think back on my life and the talk I had wit my dukes. Shit, I won't lie and say I didn't want me a little mini me running around, but a nigga was in his prime and getting this money.

"Yo!" I answered my ringing phone.

"Is that how your mama taught you to answer the phone?"

I grinned, hearing Azuri's soft voice.

"Fuck outta here, what you want?"

"See this is the shit I be talkin about wit yo ugly ass! Can't even call a nigga to see how his day is going. I swear I can't fuckin stand yo damn near purple ass Kashmir! Where the fuck is the nigga I was with last night? When yo bipolar ass decides to let him show up, then you tell him to call me!" she spazzed before hanging up on me.

Lil mama just straight snapped on a muthafucka, but I had something for her ass. I quickly busted an illegal U-turn and headed to her crib. I knew she was off work, so I was bout to pull up on her ass and give her some act right. Hanging up is a sign of disrespect and I didn't take that shit too lightly.

Parking in front of her crib, I hopped out and took the stairs two at a time before banging on the door like I was the jakes. Moments later, she swung the door open with a scowl on her pretty ass face.

"What the fuck do you want Kashmir?"

I eyed her hungrily and could tell she was fresh out the shower. The strawberries and cream body wash tickled my nose. My eyes took in the way her shorts hugged her hips and the way her breasts sat up in the tank top.

"What the fuck I tell you about yo fuckin mouth?" I asked, stepping into her space.

"Last time I fuckin checked, you are not my daddy and you don't tell me what the fuck to do!" she spat.

Instead of responding, I hemmed her little ass up and stuck my tongue down her throat. She tried to fight it a first, but she hungrily kissed me back and I pulled away.

"Shut the fuck up sometimes, you talk too got damn much," I told her, as I pushed my way into the house.

"Fix a nigga some food, I'm hungry as a muthafucka!" I called over my shoulder before sitting on the couch and turning on the tv.

She came storming into the living room and stood over me with her hands on her hips; she was mad as fuck and I was amused. If looks could kill, I would be one dead muthafucka, but her lil ass won't scaring shit this way.

"Did I fuckin stutter or some shit?" I asked her.

"Fuck you Kashmir, you better hope I don't poison yo stupid ass!" she spat before storming out.

She could talk all that shit, but guess where the fuck her ass went?

Chapter 7: Azuri

Kashmir was so lucky I low key valued his life because if I didn't, this plate of food would have rat poison all in it. After getting off of work, I cooked dinner for me and my mom but my mom was out at my auntie's house. She said she would be home in an hour or two. Thoughts of Kashmir have been on my mind all day. I called him just to see how he was doing and, of course, he answered the phone like the asshole that he is.

"Ma, where my plate at?" I finished pouring gravy over his rice before sitting his plate at the table.

"Your plate is on the table. I suggest you come eat it before it gets cold."

"Just bring it to me Azuri; the game is on."

I stopped making my plate and stomped over to him. Snatching the remote out his hand, I turned the TV off then threw the remote at him."

"The fuck is yo problem?" He sucked his teeth, sending me further into a rage.

"Kashmir, whose house are you in?" I quizzed.

"Why you askin me dumb ass questions?"

"Just answer the damn question Kashmir or you can leave."

"This your house," he answered.

"Okay, then since this is MY house, you will follow MY rules. We eat at the dinner table, not in front of the TV." I expected for him to say something smart but, instead, he got up and walked into the question.

Why can't it always be that easy? I thought to myself. I finished making my plate, poured him a cup of soda and grabbed me a bottle of water, and then sat at the table. We both dug into our food, not really saying much. I honestly wanted to ask him if he was upset with the way I talked to him. There really was no reason for me to go off on him the way I did.

"Kashmir, I just want to say-"

"Stop right there Azuri. There is no need to apologize." He smirked.

"How you know I was going to apologize?"

"I know you, ma; now, shut up so a nigga can enjoy his food."

I let out a soft laugh and finished eating. After we finished, he helped me clean up the little mess that we made. Once everything was squared away, we ended up back in the living room, catching the rest of the Spurs and Bulls game. While Kashmir was rooting for the Spurs, I had my money on the bulls. Derrick Rose was my nigga.

"Azuri, what you know 'bout ball?" Kashmir asked when the game went off. He pulled me onto his lap, causing my body to melt into his.

"What do you mean what do I know? I used to ball back in the day. You looking at Lincoln's Varsity team's point guard four years in a row," I boasted.

"Get the fuck out of here." He laughed

"Ain't nobody joking, I'm so dead ass." I jumped off his lap and walked over to my mother's wall unit. I pulled out a couple of awards, along with some photos to match. I passed them to him and giggled at his reaction.

"Damn, I got me a chick that balls, can cook, and she fine as fuck. I'ma have to call my mother and tell her a nigga done fell in love."

"You are too silly." I took everything back from him and went to go put it back. Before I could turn around, Kashmir spun me, forcing my back up against the wall.

"Kashmir, what are you doing?" I tried to steady my voice as best as I could. I didn't want him knowing he had a certain effect on me.

"Why do I have to be silly? How you know I'm not in love with you?"

"Because we just met," I replied shyly. We were centimeters away from each other. I could smell the dinner we just ate on his breath. If he got any closer, I would be able to taste it too.

"There ain't no time limit on love Azuri."

His lips grazed mine, gently kissing me, but I wanted more. I leaned up, forcing my lips against his. Throwing my arms around his neck, he began snaking his tongue in and out of my mouth. I sucked on it as if I never wanted to let it go. The feeling I was feeling was unexplainable. His kiss sent me into a euphoric high.

"Uh, excuse me, what the hell is this?" The sound of my mother's voice caused me to come down from my high. I opened my eyes and immediately pushed him away from me.

"Ma, how long have you been standing there?" I questioned. I silently prayed that Kashmir wouldn't show his ass.

"Long enough to see you trying to suck the taste buds off this young man's tongue." my mother said, causing Kashmir to laugh. I hit him in the arm, trying to get him to stop.

"I told you 'bout them hands. Watch them shits," he scolded "Hi Ms. Knox, I'm Kashmir, a friend of Azuri." It was crazy how he went from chastising me to being such a polite gentleman to my mother.

"The way your hands were all over her, I would think y'all were more than friends but you can call me Nala." She smiled, showing all thirty-two of her pearly whites. "It was nice meeting you. Hopefully, the next time I see you, we can get to know each other over dinner or something."

"I would love that." The way my mother was smiling, you would've thought she was interested in Kashmir.

"Azuri, come walk me to my car but go change first cause yo ass ain't going outside dressed like that." My mother looked from Kashmir to me, then giggled and walked away. I rolled my eyes at Kashmir and ran to my room to throw on a pair of sweats and a hoodie.

"That's more like it." He smiled, smacking me on the ass

"Whatever!"

The walk to his car was a short one and it was filled with silence. My mind was on what would have happened if my mother wouldn't have walked in. I have had sex before, so I wasn't worried about that. I was more so concerned with what would happen after we had sex.

"Come here ma." He leaned against his car and reached out for me. That obviously wasn't close enough because he yanked me into his chest.

"Why do you have to be so damn rough and you didn't have to curse in front of my mother."

"Relax, she loves a nigga, I'm good in her book. But, wassup with us? Let me know how shit is gonna be, so I can act accordingly."

"Umm, we're friends." I didn't know what else to say or what to label us.

"Iight. Go upstairs and text me when you get in the house so I know you're straight."

"Okay."

I walked back towards my building feeling some type of way. I was feeling like Kashmir dismissed me and I didn't like that feeling at all. Getting in the house, I texted him, letting him know I was in the house. His reply was good. What the fuck kind of response was good? I stared at my phone, waiting for another text to come through, but it never came. I fixed my mom a plate and then brought it to her room.

"You didn't have to bring my food in here. I was going to eat at the kitchen table."

"No, you need to relax. You been ripping and running the streets lately and I don't like it."

"Going to your aunt's house isn't ripping and running the streets, Azuri."

"To me it is."

"Enough about me. Who is this Kashmir boy you was loving on in my living room?"

"I wasn't loving on anyone and he is just a friend."

"Mhm, a friend huh? The way y'all was going at it wasn't a display of friendship."

"Ma, we are friends, nothing more." I didn't know if I was trying to convince her or myself.

"Alright, alright, no need to get feisty." My mother had her hands raised in the air like she was surrendering.

"I'm sorry, ma"

"Its fine baby, I understand. At some point, you are gonna have to allow someone to capture your heart."

"Yeah, I know ma." I sighed. I kissed her on the cheek, told her I loved her, then left out the room before she could lecture me.

I wouldn't say I had feelings for Kashmir but I liked him. Most importantly, I enjoyed his company; however, with the way his attitude was set up and the stable of bitches I knew he had, there was no way we could work. Not to mention, I didn't have time to date anyone. My life consisted of working and making sure my mother was good at all times. A love life didn't exist in the life of Azuri.

Chapter 8: Gotti

I ain't gon say that I wasn't a little slighted when Zuri said that we were just friends cause that would be a fuckin lie. That shit happened two days ago and still weighed heavy on a nigga's mind. In my mind, we were more than that, but if she couldn't see that then fuck it. Kashmir Banks ain't sweat no bitch; I didn't give a fuck who she was. Now, I ain't saying that I was cutting her off completely, but I was bout to show her ass some shit.

Today, I was having a meeting with my pops. Even though he had passed the crown down, he was still very much involved in our shit and I hated that shit sometimes.

"Why you think he wanted to see us?" Jahzir asked, passing me the blunt.

"Who the fuck knows, that's yo damn daddy," I joked.

"Fuck you bitch, he was yo daddy first," he laughed.

It was no secret that Lawrence Banks won't shit nice in the streets, but he was the same way with us too. I couldn't stand his ass sometimes, but I loved him all the same. Our relationship was rocky in the past because by me being the oldest, I saw and heard a lot of shit. Back in the day, he used to do my dukes dirty and I called him out on that shit.

I had never been one to bite my tongue about shit; I didn't give a fuck who you were. Needless to say, that muthafucka gave me my first ass whooping and schooled me at the same time.

"Late as fuckin usual," my pops spat, as soon as we walked in his office.

"Traffic was a bitch," I smirked, lying my ass off. "What you want Lawrence? Time is money," I added.

"Get fucked up in here Kash. I might be retired, but I still hand out ass whoopings when necessary," he spat.

"No disrespect pops, but I'm a grown ass man now. Leap yo ass over here and I'm gon knock you the fuck out."

He glared at me and I glared back, then broke out into a full grin before slapping it up with him. Most people didn't understand our relationship, but it wasn't meant for them to. We talked shit to each other on a daily basis; I guess you can say that's how we bonded.

"You still a rude muthafucka." He laughed.

"I learned from the best." I grinned.

"If y'all finish with this lifetime moment, can we get on with this shit. I got some pussy waitin on me!" Jahzir all but yelled.

"Shut the fuck up!" Me and Pops shouted at the same time.

Jahzir shook his head and laughed, while we sat down and got to business.

"I called y'all here today because I got some information that ain't sittin too well with me. According to my source, there's a new nigga in town from Philly named Tamir and he tryin to set up shop. He knows that you two run every inch of New York, so he put a bounty on your heads. Now, I could've handled the shit, but it ain't my place, so I just thought I would pass along the information," he said, lighting a cigar.

I sat unfazed by what he was saying. This Tamir nigga was in way over his head and he would soon realize that shit. If he knew what was good for him, he would take his ass back to Philly and be the fuck happy.

"Just keep your eyes open and put your crew on to this shit," he added.

I nodded my head and we made small talk for the next thirty minutes.

"Y'all be careful out there cause if something happens to either one of y'all, I will paint this fuckin city with blood and brain matter."

"Easy killa, we got this shit," Jah said, laughing.

"Yea, old man, don't give yourself a heart attack," I added.

"Nigga please, I'm in better shape than y'all retarded ass and I'm bout to go show your mama just how good of shape I'm in," he smirked.

"Oh hell nah. Gotti, let's get the fuck up outta here!" Jah jumped up and rushed out the door with a look of disgust on his face.

"Soft ass," Pops joked.

"Lock my door on your way out, I'm bout to go digging." He laughed.

"Chill wit that shit man," I replied.

Instead of responding, he gave me the finger and headed up the stairs while I headed for the door. After dropping Jah off to his car, I headed to my crib to chill. I wanted to call Azuri, but I didn't. Instead, I just rolled me a few blunts and played the game.

Two hours later, I was high as hell and on my fourth game when my phone chimed.

Future: I hate to bother you, but I have to close tonight and I was wondering if you could come pick me up?

Me: What time you get off friend?

Future: Midnight

Me: I'll be there friend...

I smirked a little, knowing that she just wanted to see a nigga, but I was gon go pick her little ass up and take her home. It was only a little after eight, so I decided to take a quick nap before going to pick her up.

* * * *

"You wanna take a ride with me right quick?" I asked Zena when she picked up.

"Where we going?"

"Don't fuckin worry about it, either you do or you don't, got damn!" I snapped.

"I'm sorry, I'll be ready when you get here," she softened her tone.

"Good, have yo ass outside or you gon be left!" I spat before hanging up on her ass.

Grabbing my keys, I headed out the door to get Zena and then pick up Azuri. Yea, I knew I was being childish, but I didn't give a fuck. She wanted to be friends, right? Twenty minutes later, I was pulling up on Zena, who was standing outside waiting on me. She climbed in the car and kissed my cheek before I pulled off.

"I missed you," she purred.

"Oh yea?" I asked nonchalantly.

"Yea," she replied, grabbing my dick.

"You can show me how much in a minute," I smirked.

Pulling up to McDonalds, I saw Azuri walk out and couldn't help the grin that was on my face. Even in her uniform, she was killing the game and looking good as hell. She opened the passenger door and looked shock to see Zena sitting there. Instead of making a scene, she climbed in the back and buried her head in her phone.

"What's good homie?" I asked, looking in the rearview mirror at her.

"What's up friend?" she smirked and continued to play on her phone.

"Hey girl, I'm Zena." Zena turned around and stuck her hand out.

"And?" Azuri replied, looking from her to her hand.

"Well, excuse the fuck out of me," Zena said, turning back around.

"You're excused," Azuri replied and I stifled a laugh.

Her little ass was tight and it showed all over her face, so my mission was accomplished. We pulled up to her crib and she quickly climbed out the car, but not before sticking her head back inside.

"Thanks for the ride *friend*," she said before slamming the door.

I grinned as I watched her angrily climb the steps and enter the house.

"That bitch is rude," Zena spat.

"Watch yo fuckin mouth." I glared at her.

"Well, she is," she continued.

"That's what the fuck you get for tryin to be funny and shit. She didn't give a fuck about you and quite frankly, neither do I, so come put yo face in my lap and shut the fuck up!"

She looked offended, but I didn't give a fuck; she should've kept her mouth shut. Instead of responding, she did what I said and swallowed my dick, just as my phone buzzed.

Future: Real cute Kashmir, real cute...

I didn't even respond; I just sat my phone down and headed to Zena's crib while she blew me down.

Chapter 9: Azuri

That shit Kashmir pulled was real cute. I didn't know who ole girl was but she didn't have shit on me, which was why I didn't sweat it. If it was games Kashmir wanted to play, then it was game on. But, he should have done his homework because I always played to win. Walking in the house, I checked on my mother but she was sleep. I went in my room and got settled before pulling my phone out to set my plan in motion.

"Hell must have frozen over for you to be calling me this late," Naomi laughed, while answering the phone.

"Why do you have to be so animated?"

"I'm not being animated; I'm oh so serious. When do you ever call me?"

"I'm calling you now so that's all that really matters." I was starting to second guess asking Naomi to help me out. But, without her, my plan would be pointless.

"I guess but what you want because I was about to head out."

"I need you to find out where Kashmir is going to be tomorrow night." If anyone was going to be able to find Kashmir, it was going to be Naomi.

"Wait You mean Gotti Kashmir? Kashmir, the nigga running shit? The boss Kashmir?"

"Bitch, if all of them are the same person, then yes, that's the Kashmir I'm talking about," I snapped.

"Uh huh, don't snap at me miss thing. Since you need my help, I'm going to ask all the questions I want to, especially since you wouldn't answer my phone calls after you left the game with his ass."

"Naomi, the only questions that are going to be asked is mine and I only asked you one. Can you or can you not find out where he's going to be tomorrow night? It's a Saturday, so I know his ass is going to be out somewhere."

"Tuh, I'll find out where he's going to be at on one condition."

"Naomi, what do you want, damn? You just can't do me a favor; I do them for you all the time."

"If you do me this one favor, you won't have to worry about my ass no mo."

"In that case, what's the favor?"

"Hook me up with his brother, Jahzir. That nigga is too fine."

"I'll see what I can do but I'm not making no promises."

"That's good enough for me. I'll let you know tomorrow night where they at and then I'll come scoop you. Are you off?"

"Nah, I'm off in the morning to go with mom to see the Rheumatologist, but I go in at one and work until twelve. Pick me up and then we can get ready at my house."

"Sounds good to me."

Naomi and I chatted a little longer about nothing, really. She was doing most of the talking while thoughts of Kashmir ran through my mind. I was in my feelings 'bout the way he did me and I could admit that I just wasn't going to say it to him. I wrapped up my phone call with Naomi and then went to sleep because I was going to have a long day ahead of me tomorrow.

* * * *

"So, Dr. Wright, how is everything looking?" It was time for my mother's two-week checkup. She was really supposed to go once a month, but I forced her to go twice.

"Your mother isn't out of the clear but with her taking her medicine, her symptoms are manageable, which lessens the chance of permanent damage to her organs or tissues. I think we can cut her twice a month visits to once a month. Along with taking your medicine, I feel you should start taking a yoga class. That should help with your tight joints. But for right now, she is as healthy as she can be in this situation. Make sure if anything else changes, you let me know."

"I will Dr. Wright, thank you," I told my mother's doctor.

"Before you go, I was wondering if you could tell my hard headed daughter that it is okay for me to go back to work," my mother said before the doctor could walk out the room.

"It is okay for you to work no more than three days. I don't want you to overwork your body. Also, make sure that your job is indoors and not outdoors."

"Okay, thank you." My mother smiled before turning her attention to me.

"Ma, don't even start," I told her.

"You told me you wanted the doctor to say it for your ears to hear. Now that he did and you heard it, I'm going back to work. Even if it's only for three days, at least then you will be able to have two days off, instead of one."

I didn't even bother arguing with my mother. I let her have her way on this one but if I started to see the slightest change in her, I was making her quit. I made sure my mom got in the house before I walked the twenty blocks to work. Before clocking in, I made sure to text Naomi to make sure we were still on tonight. She texted me back saying she would be there.

Instead of work flying by liked I hoped, the shit dragged, so when it was time to clock out, my ass hopped, skipped, and jumped out of that door. Walking through the parking lot, I checked my phone for the tenth time to see if Kashmir had called or text me. Of course, his ass didn't, which made me want to go through with the plan even more.

"Hurry your ass up before we late to the party!" Naomi yelled, honking her horn. I shot her the middle finger and continued to take my time towards her car.

"I'm not rushing. I just worked an eleven-hour shift, a bish is tired," I spat, finally reaching her car.

"I don't even know why I agreed to help your annoying ass," she sassed, while pulling off.

"You agreed to help me because you think you're getting something out of it."

"I don't think, I know. You still haven't told me what's going on with you and Kashmir though. I need to know how you swung that."

"And I'm not going to tell you because there is nothing to tell."

"Yeah, okay. The way that nigga dissed me for you tells me everything I need to know."

I turned the radio up, drowning out the conversation Naomi was trying to have. We pulled up to my house in no time. Getting out, Naomi was still talking about how we were going to shut Club Exclusive down. I paid her ass no mind because I was the least bit interested in the club; I had one purpose and one purpose only.

Naomi was already dressed and I was happy about that. I quickly showered and lotioned my body. Looking at the outfit Naomi had picked out for me, I was starting to have second thoughts. She picked me up a black lace nude illusion keyhole back jumpsuit. While trying to make my decision, a text came through on my phone.

Kashmir: Wassup FRIEND

It was from Kashmir and the text alone helped me to make up my decision. I threw the jumpsuit on and gave myself the once over in my floor length mirror. At a quick glance, you would think the lace was the only material I was wearing. I did a quick little turn and I had to admit, I was killing this jumpsuit. It fit my body like a glove.

"Damn girl, who would've known you was working with all of that," Naomi cooed, coming in the room.

"Shut up before you wake my mother," I told her.

"Girl, your mama is knocked out but come on because I'm ready to go."

I slipped my black pumps on, sprayed my body spray, and handed my phone to Naomi to take a quick pick. I posed, making sure the little cake I was working with poked out in the picture. Naomi handed me back my phone and I sent the picture to Kashmir with the caption. 'Headed out friend can't talk 'bout to shut shit down.' I turned my phone off, throwing it on my bed.

"Why are you leaving your phone?"

"I don't want any interruptions." I smiled.

"Well, I just got word Gotti is at the club, so let's go."

I followed her out the house, ready to get my night started. I would bet my bottom dollar Kashmir was blowing my phone up. It was cool though because that picture was nothing compared to how I was going to show my ass at this club.

Chapter 10: Gotti

Azuri knew how to fuckin get under my skin, but it was cool though. If she wanted to keep playing this game, then she could go right ahead. Once she sent me that fuckin picture, a nigga was ready to put my foot in her ass. Apparently, she had turned her phone off, so I said fuck it; I would see her ass around.

Tonight, me and my niggas were turning it up at Exclusive. I rarely went out, but when I did, it was a turn up situation. We had all the essentials in our VIP area; bottles, blunts, and bad bitches. I was kicked back drinking D'Usse straight from the bottle, while a bad ass brown skin grinded on my lap.

She was cute and shit, but she wasn't Azuri, so I was quickly becoming bored with her ass.

"Aye Gotti!" I heard Jahzir shout.

Turning my attention to him, he motioned for me to come here, so I tapped lil mama on the ass for her to move and made my way to him.

"Ain't that ya girl?" he asked, nodding toward the bar downstairs.

My blood boiled at the sight of her at the bar, grinning while some nigga spit game in her ear. I couldn't front though, she was looking good as hell and wearing the fuck outta that jumpsuit.

"What you wanna do?" Jah asked.

"Not shit, fuck that bitch," I spat.

Jah looked at me in surprise and I even shocked myself with the words I spoke. Chasing Azuri was a fuckin full time job and I ain't have time for that shit. If she ain't want to fuck wit a nigga, I wasn't gon force her ass. It was too many bitches out here that would love to get next to Kashmir Banks for me to be running behind one.

"You sure?" he asked.

Eyeing her once more, she looked up and her eyes met mine. I stared at her blankly before giving her a smirk and turning away.

"Yea, I'm good." I shrugged and made my way back to shorty.

Pulling her off the couch, I placed her back on my lap and she started dancing again. I ain't gon lie; a part of me wanted to go down there and snatch Azuri's little ass up. But, I already knew she was doing this shit to get back at me for the shit I pulled with Zena the other day.

I was too grown to play this tit for tat shit; either she was gon fuck wit a nigga or she wasn't, simple as that. I knew what I said to Jah, but I wasn't sure if I meant that shit; my ego was just a little bruised.

August Alsina's *No Love* started to play in the club and I nodded my head to the music. Shorty told me she was going to the bathroom and I shrugged, not really caring either way cause I had Azuri's lil ass on my brain. Getting out my seat, I stood at the balcony and my eyes landed on her, dancing with the lame nigga from the bar.

Like a magnetic pull, I was drawn to her as her eyes quickly landed on mine. We stared each other down with intensity, neither backing down, then she started rapping Nicki Minaj's part.

August you know, I'm here to save you/Me and them

girls, we ain't the same, boo

You know I hate it, when you leave me/ 'Cause you love it then you leave it

But you know how bad I need it/You so fuckin'

conceited/Why you coming over weeded...

I eyed her with a smirk cause she was dancing with ol buddy, but her eyes were fixated on me.

You can't treat me like you treat them/Yes, I am the crème de la crème/Yes I am from one to ten, ten You fronting in them streets, keep saying we just friends/You can't front like this ain't way realer

I know you hard, I know that you a killer/I know you

started off a dope dealer

But let your guard down, your niggas know you feel her, feel her

So what you want, baby?

I mouthed the words, *All I want is you, so what you tryin do?*

She cracked a small grin and my heart skipped a beat. I knew what I said earlier, but fuck all that shit, Azuri was mine and that's just what the fuck it was. Tossing back my drink, I sat my cup down on the table and made my way down the stairs.

Bitches were grinning and niggas were trying to dap me up, but I was on a mission; I was going to get my girl. I pulled her away from ol buddy and into my chest, just staring in her eyes.

"Aye, my man, we was dancing," the fuck nigga said.

"My nigga, if you want to make it home tonight, I suggest you get the fuck on!" I said, loud enough for him to hear, but I kept my eyes on Azuri.

"Let me go Kashmir, I was dancing!" she snapped.

Getting closer to her, I brought my face down by her ear. "Don't make me fuckin embarrass you in here Azuri. You already testing my patience by even being here with this shit on. I'm done playin this game wit yo simple ass, so right now, I need you to make a fuckin choice. Either you gon fuck wit a nigga or we gon go our separate ways, but I ain't bout to keep doin kiddie shit."

She looked at me in shock before anger flashed in her eyes. "You started this shit Kashmir, so I decided to join the fuckin game! Obviously, you wasn't to fucked up about me because you brought that bum bitch wit you to my job. So, who's really playin games? Then you come over here givin me a got damn ultimatum like I'm a fuckin child; nigga, you got me fucked up!" she spat angrily.

Before I could respond, the fuck nigga, who I didn't even know was standing there, grabbed Azuri and I blanked, knocking his ass out cold.

"Let's fuckin go Azuri!" I spat, grabbing her hand.

She pulled away from me and glared at me.

"I didn't come here wit you and I ain't leavin wit you! Fuck you, Kashmir!"

"Word? It's fuck me Zuri? That's how you feel ma?" I asked, getting in her face.

We were so close; I could smell the amaretto sour on her breath. She didn't respond; she just glared at me. Nodding my head, I smirked and took a step back.

"Grow the fuck up Azuri, I'll see you around ma," I told her before walking away.

I headed back to VIP, grabbed ol girl that was grinding on my lap, dapped up my niggas, and headed back down the stairs. Azuri was at the bar with Naomi's old trashbox ass, but stopped her conversation when she saw me and ol girl walking her way. She downed her drink and stepped in my path before turning her attention to ol girl.

"He won't be needing you tonight," she told her.

On the inside, a nigga was smiling like hell, but on the outside, I played that shit cool.

"Excuse me?"

"Bitch, I know it may be a little loud in here, but I know damn well you just heard what the fuck I said. You see, this nigga standing right here, that's me; we just had a little miscommunication. So, what I need for you to do is go find you another dick to stick down your throat for tonight, cause this one is occupied."

I ain't gon front, seeing Azuri boss up on ol girl like that had my dick hard.

"Gotti, who is this?" Ol girl turned and asked me.

"The first lady of the streets," I smirked and let her hand go.

Azuri made her way to me and wrapped her arms around my neck, pulling me in for a kiss and sticking her tongue down my throat. I grabbed her ass and squeezed it gently before breaking our kiss.

"I'm ready to go," she told me.

Nodding my head, I grabbed her hand and, together, we walked out the club, leaving ol girl standing there looking stupid.

When we got outside, I helped her into my truck and her little ass flipped the script.

"You goin home wit me?" I asked her.

"Fuck no, I'm goin home," she replied, looking out the window.

"Word?" I asked in shock.

"Did you not understand me? I'm going home Kashmir, what you thought because of that little performance that we were gon be straight? Nah, it don't work like that. You shut down my fun, so I shut down yours." She shrugged.

I chuckled lightly cause her little ass was a trip. But instead of responding, I headed in the direction of her house. Twenty minutes later, we were pulling up and she tried to hop out.

"So, that's it? A nigga don't get a goodnight or a kiss?" I asked her.

"Let me clear this up for you so we don't have to revisit this topic again. I'm not like these other bitches out here; I don't give a fuck what you have or who you are. I'm not gon bust it wide open for you because you're the king of the streets. Do I like you? Absolutely, but I *love* me and most of all, I respect me. You're right though, this game we're playing is getting old and childish. If you want me to be with you, then prove it to me, actions always speak louder than words. Now goodnight, *friend*," she smirked before getting out the truck.

She had my black ass on stuck, but I could only respect the shit that she said. If I didn't know it before, I knew now that Azuri was a different breed and I would have to treat her as such. The conversation I had with my mother replayed in my head, so I was gonna take her advice.

Chapter 11: Azuri

She said, I don't want a model, I don't want a movie star. You don't have to win the lotto, oh I want you to win my heart. She said I just want someone true. She said I just want someone to smoke with me babe and lay with me babe. And laugh with me babe, I just want the simple things.

The soft sound of Miguel's voice singing caused me to stir in my sleep. Without opening my eyes, I reached over to my phone, hitting the snooze button. I was tired as hell and didn't really feel like going to work, especially after I got home at four in the morning. Still lying down, I tried pulling myself together before the next alarm went off. I blamed me being tired on Kashmir. If his ass wasn't playing games, then I wouldn't have gone out last night knowing I had to be up at six the next morning. Miguel's singing the second time caused me to get my ass out of bed. I let the song play out because it was one of my favorites. Miguel and Chris Brown took turns singing about how it was the simplest things they wanted out of their significant other.

It kind of reminded me of Kashmir in a way. All I wanted from him was his time and attention; the simple things. For some reason, he couldn't grasp that concept. I didn't know what his past girls were like, but I wasn't nothing like them. I quickly turned the song off at Future's part because it was too early to be this emotional. I took a quick twenty-minute shower before getting dressed. I packed my uniform in my bag, then went into the kitchen to have breakfast with my mother.

"Hey baby, where did you go last night?" she asked, sitting a plate of French toast in front of me.

"I went out with Naomi. How did you know I left out?"

"You know Naomi has a big ass mouth. She woke me up a couple of times; I was just too tired to tell her ass to shut up. I'm happy you got out, you deserve to have some fun."

"I wouldn't consider what happened last night fun but I guess." I shrugged, cutting into my French toast.

"What happened last night?"

I ran down the events that happened between Kashmir and I. When I was finished, my mother just looked at me, shaking her head like I did something wrong.

"Why are you shaking your head at me?"

"I'm shaking my head because you allowed that young man to pull you off your square. You allowed him to take you out of your element. Baby, I know I taught you that you can't ever win the game when you're playing on someone else's field."

"It doesn't even matter because I'm done playing the back and forth game; it's childish as hell. If he wants to be with me, then he needs to show it or just come out and say it."

"Have you told him that you want to be with him?"

"No, why do I have to be the one to tell him I want to be with him? He already knows that I like him. I think that's enough."

"Baby, that's your problem right there. You say you are over the games but you are still playing them. If you want to be with him, then you need tell him, just like you expect him to tell you I'm sure he expects the same thing in return. Relationships are all about communication and, right now, the both of y'all got it fucked up."

"Ma, it's too early to be trying to drop gems on me." I laughed, trying to lighten the mood.

"It's never too early. But you go ahead and go to work and think about what I said."

I finished up my breakfast, then gave my mother a kiss, letting her know that I loved her before running out the door. I wasn't in the mood to walk, so I jumped in a two-dollar cab. The cab ride was a short one but it gave me time to think about what my mother said. My mother had a point; communication was important in a relationship. I just wasn't the one with the problem, Kashmir was. So, if he wanted to make things official between us, then he would have to speak up or forever hold his peace and be okay with us being friends.

I got out the cab, paid my two dollars, and was about to walk into work when a text came through on my phone.

Kashmir (Asshole): Good morning beautiful.

I blushed at the text because it wasn't one that I expected. I replied back, telling him good morning and that I was on my way into work. By the time I changed clothes, Kashmir still hadn't sent a text back. I shrugged my shoulders, threw my phone in my locker, and clocked in for work. The good morning text I received still had me smiling when I made it to my register.

* * * *

When it was time for me to take my break, I couldn't have been happier. I clocked out and walked out the door, ready to go get some oxtails from the Golden Crust up the street.

"Ayo sexy!" I heard someone call out.

I didn't bother to turn around or anything because I was hungry and my break was only thirty minutes.

"It's like that; you don't even recognize your man's voice anymore." At the mention of my man's voice, I turned around to see Kashmir jogging up to me.

"Last time I checked, you were my friend, not my man." I smiled.

"Yeah, whatever ma. Where you off too?"

"To get something to eat from Golden Crust. What are you doing out here?"

"I came to see what time you got off." He grabbed me by my pant loops, pulling me closer to him.

"You could've just sent me a text, you know. You didn't have to come all the way out here."

"My phone died while I was handling business. Let me find out you not happy to see me and shit." He slightly pushed me away, acting as if he was hurt or something.

"I don't know how I feel about seeing you but I get off at six."

"Damn, when I texted you, it was like seven in the morning. They got you doing doubles and shit."

"They don't have me doing anything. I choose to do it," I sassed. The way he said it slightly offended me, for some reason.

"I didn't mean nothing by that, ma. Look, I'm coming to pick you up around eight; we need to talk about a few things."

"Ummm, I don't know..." I said, playing it off like I had other plans but in reality, I was free because I was off tomorrow.

"I wasn't giving your ass an option. I'm picking your big headed ass up and that's final. Now, give me kiss and go get your food. I can't have my future out here hungry and shit."

I giggled at what he said and leaned up to give him a kiss. As our lips parted, he stuck his tongue in my mouth. I sucked on it, gently tasting the winter fresh gum he must've been chewing on. When the kiss started to get deeper and more intense, I pulled away.

"We are only friends Kashmir and friends don't do that."

"Yeah iight, whatever Azuri, just have your ass outside when I pull up," he smirked, while swaging away.

I continued walking to Golden Crust, thinking about what Kashmir said. What did we have to talk about? Maybe he was finally coming to his senses and was gonna tell me what it is between us. Whatever it was he wanted to talk about, I was anxious to find out but, more importantly, I was happy at the fact I was just going to be around him. It was the simple things.

Chapter 12: Gotti

After I left Azuri, I headed to the barbershop to get my shit lined up, then I hit the mall wit my dukes. I had a special night planned for Azuri; I was tired of the back and forth shit with her. Either she was gon rock wit a nigga or she wasn't, it was that simple.

"What you think about this Kashy?" my mom asked, holding up a bad ass blue dress.

"I'm feelin that shit ma." I nodded.

"I know you better watch yo got damn mouth!" she snapped.

"My bad ma." I laughed.

She found some shoes and we headed to the counter to pay for it. Once we were done, I headed to the jewelry store to pick up Azuri's gift. The shit set me back a couple stacks, but she was worth it; plus, that shit was fly as hell.

I got lunch with my dukes and then dropped her off before heading to Azuri's house. I knew that she was at work for the next two hours, but I was hoping that her mom was home. Thirty minutes later, I was knocking on the door.

"Hey, Kashmir right? Azuri isn't home, she's at work until six," her mom told me.

"I know Ms. Knox, I actually came by to see you," I replied.

She looked surprised, but invited me in and led me to the living room.

"What can I do for you, son?"

"Well, Ms. Knox, I'm sure that Azuri has told you about our back and forth relationship. She told me the other night to show her that I wanted to be with her, so that's what I'm going to do. I like her a lot and I feel like she's the one for me; I just gotta prove it to her. I set up a little date for us tonight, so I need you to put this stuff on her bed and I'll be here at eight to pick her up," I explained.

"Yes, she has told me about the games you two are playing with each other. Now, you're not the ideal candidate I had for my daughter because I can tell that you're in the streets, but I can also sense that you're a good guy. All I want for my daughter is for her to be happy and live life. She's devoted so much of her time to me that she forgot to live and I don't like that. Now, if you're serious about her, then I'll help you, but if you aren't, then leave her be."

"With all due respect, if I wasn't serious about Azuri, I never would've pursued her. I have chicks throwing themselves at me daily, but Azuri is different; she's what I need in my life. We argue like crazy, but at the same time, we just vibe. I'm willing to do whatever I have to do to get her."

"Well then son, she'll be ready at eight. But know this, if you hurt my daughter, I will personally whoop yo ass. Don't let the soft voice and cute face fool you; I go hard for mine," she said, looking at me sternly.

I laughed a bit, cause I could see where Azuri got her attitude from.

"Azuri is a good girl; she's just a little stubborn and it might take a while to knock down those walls. But if you're really up for the challenge, then be patient with her and don't try to force anything on her," she added.

I nodded my head and, for the next hour, we sat talking. Azuri's dukes was cool as hell and I could tell that she only wanted what was best for her daughter. I couldn't do nothing but respect that.

Two hours later, I was looking at myself in the full length mirror and I had to admit that a nigga was handsome; standing at 6'2" dark chocolate skin, muscular build with light brown eyes, and pearly white teeth. Tonight, I was donned in a dark blue button up, gray slacks, and blue and gray Gucci loafers.

A nigga was killing the game and that wasn't me being cocky; shit, that was a nigga speaking facts. Spraying some Curve cologne on, I slipped on my watch and chain, then headed downstairs. Since I was on my grown man shit tonight, I decided to pull out my smoke gray Cadillac CTS-V.

I slid some Jahiem into the CD player and headed to pick up my future. I pulled up to her building, grabbed the pink roses from the front seat, and made my way inside. I knocked on the door and waited; her mother answered moments later.

"Well, don't you look handsome." She smiled.

"Thank you Ms. Knox," I replied.

"Hush that Ms. Knox mess up, I told you to call me Nala," she said, ushering me inside.

"No disrespect, but my mother would whoop my ass if she heard me addressing you by your first name," I told her.

Before she could respond, Azuri appeared and, I swear, a nigga's heart skipped a few beats. She looked stunning in the dress that my mom had picked out, her hair was full of soft curls, and minimal makeup donned her face.

"Damn," I mumbled under my breath.

Her eyes lit up when I handed her the flowers; she smelled them and thanked me before handing them to her mother.

"You two enjoy yourselves and Azuri, text me if you're not coming home," she told her.

"Oh, I'll be coming home," Azuri replied.

I didn't bother responding. I just smirked at her mother, who winked at me in return. Ushering Azuri out the door, we walked hand in hand to my car and I helped her inside.

"What has gotten into you?" she asked as I pulled onto the street.

"Show and prove, right?"

She nodded her head and sung along to Jaheim as he talked about what she really means. Her head bobbed as I stole glances at her as she sung the end of the chorus.

You gotta read between the lines and see

You gotta go where no man's gone before

You gotta reach real deep inside her dreams

And that's when you'll find out what she really means...

We made minimal small talk until we pulled up to the Bouley Restaurant in Tribeca. I had never been here, but my dukes suggested it, so I was just gon rock wit it and hoped she liked the shit.

I pulled up to the valet and helped Azuri out the car, taking in the way that dress was hugging all her curves.

Walking into the restaurant, I gave them my name and they immediately escorted us to a private dining area in the back.

"Your server will be with you shortly, enjoy your evening," the hostess said before disappearing.

"This restaurant is... fancy," Azuri said, looking around.

"Only the best for my girl." I winked.

"I'm not your girl," she smirked.

"Not yet," I smirked back.

She shook her head and opened her menu; her eyes bucked at the prices.

"Kashmir, have you lost yo black ass mind? Have you seen the prices of this shit?" she asked in a harsh whisper.

"It's cool Azuri, just order whatever you want." I shrugged.

"No Kashmir, this is ridiculous and half of this shit I can't even pronounce! I would've been perfectly fine getting a hot dog or pizza from Coney Island."

I knew then that she was a keeper. Most bitches would've been trying to order the most expensive shit on the menu, but her little ass was trying to leave.

"Would you feel better if we went back to my crib and ordered takeout?" I asked her.

She hit me with the side eye and I chuckled lightly.

"Nothing more ma, just eat and chill," I told her with my hands raised.

"Nothing more," she said sternly.

I nodded my head, threw some bills on the table, and we left out. While we were waiting for the valet to bring my car around, I just stared at her. I didn't know what the fuck Azuri was doing to me, but she had a nigga's head gone.

A nigga ain't never did no shit like this for a chick, but she made me want to be different, she made me want to be better. We took the twenty-minute ride to my house in silence. Twenty minutes later, we were pulling up and I helped her out the car.

"Wow, your house is gorgeous," she told me.

"Thanks," I replied nonchalantly.

I had been living here for the past year but to me it was nothing more than a house. Half of the time, I didn't even stay here; I stayed at my condo in the city. She kicked off her heels and walked around, giving herself a tour.

"Damn, make yourself at home and shit," I smirked.

"We been having a good night so far, don't ruin that," she said, rolling her eyes.

"Don't get fucked up behind that mouth Azuri," I threatened.

She waved me off and headed up the stairs, while I shook my head and followed. Entering my bedroom, I tossed my shirt to the side and stepped out of my shoes and slacks.

"You could've waited until I left the room to do all that," she sassed.

"For what? This shit belong to you anyway, sooner or later I'm gon put this dick in your life." I grinned, grabbing my dick and licking my lips.

"You're such an ass," she said, turning to walk out the bedroom.

"You like that shit though," I replied.

Once I changed my clothes, I laid out a pair of shorts and a tank top for her, then told her to change while I ordered the food.

"Here, I meant to give this to your earlier," I said, handing her the gift box while we were lying across my bed talking.

She opened it and her mouth dropped. I had my jeweler do a custom piece for me. It was a twenty-four karat chain and attached to it was a diamond encrusted A going through the letter K.

"Kashmir, I can't take this," she protested.

"You can and you will," I told her, taking it from her and putting it on her. "This so niggas can know who you belong to," I added.

"Nigga, I don't belong to you," she snapped.

"Got damn Azuri, can you ever just go wit the fuckin flow? A nigga can't even do nothin nice for yo simple ass wit out you bitchin!"

"Nigga, did you just call me a bitch?" she asked, standing up.

I ran my hand over my face and bit my lip to calm myself down.

"Did you hear me call you a bitch? I said bitchin, there's a difference," I replied.

"See, this is why this shit ain't gon work, you disrespectful as fuck!" she said, mushing my forehead.

"Watch that shit Azuri, make me yoke yo lil ass up!"

"What the fuck ever, take me home!"

"Hell fuckin no, you wanna leave, then you better beat them fuckin feet!" I said, flipping through the channels.

She huffed and puffed, but I igged her simple ass. I lived a good forty minutes from Coney Island, so I knew she wasn't gon walk and a cab was gon set her back a grip. I watched in amusement as she flopped down next to me and folded her arms.

"I thought you was leavin?" I asked, grinning.

"Don't say shit to me Kashmir, just find us a movie and shut the fuck up!"

"Aye, yo lil ass ain't gon keep tryin to boss up on me and shit, make me give yo ass some act right!" I told her.

"You need a Snickers or some shit? Cause you're not yourself when you're hungry." I laughed.

She ignored me, but stifled a laugh and gnawed on her bottom lip; her little ass was really mad and over nothing at that. Shaking my head, I settled on *How High* and got comfortable as we waited on the food.

Chapter 13: Azuri

The Chinese food came about twenty minutes into the movie. Kashmir handed me my shrimp and broccoli and went back towards the top of the bed. I sat Indian style eating my food and trying to watch the movie, but my mind wasn't there. The little argument I had with Kashmir kept replaying. I felt bad for the way I was snapping at him, especially when he was only trying to do something nice for me. Kashmir was an asshole for sure but he wasn't that bad of a guy. If I wanted him to stop snapping on me, I would have to stop snapping on him as well. I grabbed the remote that was next to me, muted the TV, and spun around facing him.

"The fuck yo little ass mute the movie for?" This was one of the reasons why I always snapped on his punk ass.

"I'm just trying to talk to you. Is that okay?"

"Wassup Zuri, what you want to talk about?" He sat his food down, crossed his arms, then began to stare at me. The look he was giving me was so intense.

"I, uh, want to say sorry for how I, uh, went off on you." The apology came out choppy instead of smooth.

"Come here Azuri!"

I stuffed more broccoli and shrimp in my mouth before sitting it on the nightstand. I sat in between his legs but that wasn't where he wanted me. He lifted me up, sitting me on his lap so I was straddling him.

"Talk to me, Azuri."

"Talk to you about what?" I asked shyly.

"Wassup with all this hostility between us. Even when I'm trying to do something nice for yo ass, I still get snapped at."

"So, it's okay for you to snap but when-"

"Nah, don't even try to feed me that bullshit ma. Just cause I handle yo small ass a certain way doesn't mean you try and handle me the same. Nix that shit you were about to say and keep it eight more than ninety-two with me, Azuri."

I stared into his eyes as he looked back into mine. I was feeling Kashmir but he had the potential to hurt me. If hurting me wasn't enough, he had the potential to cause me to lose focus on everything that I had going on. At the moment, I didn't quite know who I was because my mother was always my first priority. With Kashmir coming into the picture, he demanded time and attention; two things I barely had for myself. I would hate to take things all the way with him and lose myself in him and my mother.

"It's either you can tell me what the fuck is up or you can go ma?"

"You always trying to kick someone out of something." I giggled.

"This isn't even a laughing matter right now."

"Okay, Kashmir, okay. I snap at you and go off because it keeps you from getting close to me."

"Yo, if you didn't want me around, then that's all you needed to say." His nostrils began to flare and he tried to push me off of him. I quickly wrapped my arms around his neck because he wasn't just going to up and leave when I was finally opening up to his dumbass.

"Get the fuck off me, Zuri. You don't want me gettin close to your stankin ass, then I'm gone."

"How are you leaving when you live here?" I questioned, still holding on for dear life.

"You right ma, get the fuck out!" he barked.

"I'm not going anywhere so all that yelling you're doing is for the birds. You want me to keep it a buck with you but as soon as I do, you want to start getting emotional and shit. Now, shut the fuck up and listen to what I have to say. If you still want me to leave after I say what needs to be said, then that's cool. For now, though, just listen."

"Azuri, watch your fuckin' mouth!"

I rolled my eyes at him and kissed him lightly on his lips. "As I was saying, I go off on you the way I do to keep you from getting close. I never go too far because I want you around. I know it sounds dumb as hell but it's the truth. Since I graduated high school, I devoted all of my time to my mother. I'm not complaining because I love my mother to death and I would do anything for her. It's just that I haven't really figured out who I am as a woman. Being with you demands a lot of time and attention and I don't have much of either. What I'm trying to say is that I'm scared of taking things further with you because between you and my mother, when will I ever have time for myself? How can I be the type of woman you want and need when I don't even know the type of woman I am?" A couple of tears fell but I quickly wiped them away. There was no way in hell I was going to let him see me cry because then I would never hear the end of it.

"Azuri, the type of woman that you are is very rare in this generation. The type of woman you are is selfless and that's one of the things I admire about you. Not a lot of females would put their dreams on hold for their mother. But, you did it because you're different. You are in a league of your own and that's all that matters. You think these other hoes out here know what type of woman they are? If you think they do, then you wrong. The only thing they know is which nigga got the biggest bank roll and longest dick, which is me, but that's a conversation for another day." He laughed. I giggled with him, mushing him in the face.

"Nah, seriously though Azuri. I haven't known you for long but I see the type of woman you are, and that's exactly the type of woman I need and want. Even if you don't see it ma, you're spectacular in my eyes." I saw nothing but sincerity in his eyes as he spoke each word. It felt as time stopped and we were in a world of our own.

"Did yo thug ass just say spectacular?" I laughed. The moment we were sharing was getting a little too deep for me.

"What, a nigga can't be an intelligent thug?" he asked, cocking his head to the side.

"You can be whatever you want as long as your mine at the end of the day." I realized what I just said and covered my mouth, trying to stop myself from saying anything else.

"Ma, did you just ask me out? I thought that was my job and shit, but I'm flattered." He faked blushed, causing me to really blush.

"Didn't nobody ask yo stupid ass out. It was a joke. See, haha." I tried to laugh but it wasn't convincing at all.

"Azuri, if you want me to be yo nigga, then just say the word. In my eyes, you are already mine, so it's only right I'm yours."

"Then if I'm yours and you're mine, what do we need to talk about it for? What's understood doesn't need to be explained," I told him.

"Nah, I'm not one of those niggas. When a nigga says that shit, it's because he don't really want to fuck with a chick. He doesn't want to claim her in the streets, so he spits that line. I'm not that dude. Azuri, you're mine and I want the world to know it. I never hid shit before and I'm not 'bout to start now. You're my queen and trust me when I say, the streets will know it."

"Damn!" was all I was able to say. There was more to Kashmir then what I thought. I honestly thought he would be down with the what's understood doesn't need to be explained shit. I obviously was wrong.

"Yeah, damn is right; now, claim yo nigga before I call a bitch over that wouldn't mind claimin me," he smirked cockily.

"Kashmir, don't get fuck up. You're mine; it's as simple as that. All them bitches that's in your phone need to get deleted now."

"Azuri baby, you don't got nothing to worry about. You fucking with a real boss ma. Shit, I thought you knew." He passed me his phone and unlocked it.

I scrolled through his contacts and there were no females' names saved in his phone. I didn't even see my name. I looked at his text messages and there wasn't any unsaved numbers or females' names in there either.

"Okay, so where is my name?"

"Look under Future."

I scrolled to the name Future and hit the button and my number was sure enough there. A goofy ass smile spread across my face.

"Azuri, all I see is you, ma." I leaned over and kissed him.

"Iight, enough of all this mushy shit, let's finish watching the movie.

He spun me around, so I was facing the TV, and rested my head on his chest. Once again, I tried to watch the movie but my mind wasn't there. My mind was too busy thinking about what the future held for Kashmir and I.

Chapter 14: Gotti

It had been two months since I made it official with Azuri and shit had been sweet between us. Being with her was like a breath of fresh air and a nigga wasn't even snapping as much as I used to. Don't get me wrong, I was still an asshole, but it wasn't as bad as before.

My dukes was stressing me about bringing Azuri to dinner, so I finally gave in. I just hoped my pops was on his best behavior. I was also gon talk to my dukes about hiring Azuri in her shoe store cause I couldn't have my girl working at Mickey D's, fuck that shit.

If it was up to me, her little ass wouldn't work, but I liked the fact that she was on her independent shit. I had even offered to pay her mother's bills up for a year, but she shut that shit the fuck down. Me being me though, I paid the shit up anyway. I was just preparing myself for the backlash that was gon come from Azuri.

The downside to our relationship was that Azuri wasn't coming up off the pussy. Don't get me wrong; a nigga had willpower and shit, but got damn. I was gon have blue balls fuckin wit her lil ass. The old me wanted to say fuck it and let one of these bitches suck my dick, but I wasn't even trying to lose Azuri over no bullshit ass nut.

"Aye nigga, fuck you over there daydreamin about and shit?" Dru asked me.

"How I fucked yo dukes last night nigga," I joked.

Everybody laughed except Dru, who just shot me the finger. We were posted up on the block, while I watched these niggas waste money shooting dice. It was the first week of June and hot as a son of a bitch outside. The block was full, hoes had next to nothing on, and niggas posted up trying to look hard.

"Hey Gotti." I heard from behind me.

I sucked my teeth and ignored her ass; I knew Naomi's voice from anywhere.

"Damn, it's like that?" she asked with attitude, walking into my view.

"It's been like that, fuck you thought?" I asked, mugging her ass.

Her ass was damn near naked out her in a pair of shorts that had her ass hanging out and what looked like a bathing suit top with her titties spilling out the top. Shaking my head, I focused my attention back on the dice game.

"We damn near family now nigga, so you gon be around me," she snapped.

"Not hardly, Zuri don't even fuck wit yo ass like that and even if she did, I still wouldn't fuck wit yo trout faced thot ass," I spat.

She flipped me off and sucked her teeth before turning her attention to Jahzir.

"Hey Jah," she said, licking her lips.

"Sup," he replied, hitting her with the head nod.

"You," she told him.

He chuckled lightly and shook his head. She was definitely barking up the wrong tree cause Jah had a lady and her ass was crazy as fuck. A lot of people didn't know about Megan cause she wasn't from round here, but the ones who did, knew she would turn up on Jah in a heartbeat.

"When we gon kick it?" she asked him.

"Look here baby girl, I got a lady and even if I didn't, I still wouldn't fuck wit you. Your reputation is fucked up in every borough and city in NY, so I'm good on that shit. I heard yo mouth game was super, but I'll pass, cause ain't no tellin what the fuck you got in yo throat," he told her.

Shaking my head, I chuckled under my breath. Shit, Jah was the laid back one, but he would embarrass the fuck outta yo ass too.

"No wonder y'all brothers, both of you niggas is rude as fuck!" she spat angrily.

"Don't be mad at us cause the hood got a hoe fax on yo ass!" I shouted after her, causing everybody to laugh.

"Y'all hell man, leave Naomi alone," Dru spoke up.

I looked at his ass with the side eye and cocked my head slightly.

"You want that bitch, don't you?" Jah asked before I could.

"I mean, shorty a fuckin dime and I think I could be the nigga that changed her life," he replied.

"Be my guest nigga, but make sure you take her ass to the clinic and have them run every test known to mankind." I laughed.

"Shit, it's a good thing nobody in our circle fucked her ass." Jah laughed.

Dru gave us all the finger and went back to the dice game. I chopped it up with them for the next hour, until it was time to pick up my baby from work.

Pulling up to her job, I smiled when I saw her walking out the door. Azuri didn't even know she had a nigga; she did what no other bitch had ever done and that was capture the heart of Kashmir Banks.

"Hey friend," she joked, hopping in the car.

"Don't play wit me, Azuri," I said, giving her ass a stern look.

"Ok, I'm just kidding," she giggled. "Hey punkin." She smiled before kissing my lips.

"The fuck is a punkin?" I asked.

"You, you're my punkin pie," she replied, grinning widely.

"Yo, you corny as fuck yo." I laughed.

"You like it though," she said, sticking out her tongue.

"Keep openin yo mouth like that and I'm gon slide somethin in it," I smirked.

"Nasty ass," she said, rolling her eyes.

I headed toward my house, so her little ass could get ready. She had more clothes than a little bit at my house and I could tell her dukes was glad she was out more than she was home. I understood Azuri's concern for her mother, but she needed to ease up a little bit.

"So, what's your mother like?" she asked me.

"Dukes is cool, she real laid back, but she gangsta as fuck too." I laughed. "Pops, on the other hand, has absolutely no filter; he don't give a fuck what come out his mouth," I added.

"So, basically he's an older version of you," she smirked.

"Yea aight." I laughed.

* * * *

"Ma, this is Azuri; Azuri, this is my mother, Gina," I introduced the two.

"Nice to meet you, Mrs. Banks." Azuri smiled.

"Girl, I ain't that damn old, call me Mama or call me Gina." She smiled, pulling her into a hug.

"She's pretty Kashy, you did good son," she told me.

Azuri blushed slightly and looked at me; I blew her a kiss and winked at her. We made our way into the living room. I shook my head when I saw my pops.

"What's up lil nigga, who that you got wit you?" he asked, once he noticed us.

"Azuri, this nigga right here is my pops Lawrence," I told her.

"Nice to meet you, sir." She smiled.

"Sir? Oh, you got you a broad with some manners huh? Bout time, cause Lord knows this fuckin nigga don't got none." He smirked.

He got up and pulled Azuri in for a hug before kissing her cheek.

"Aye nigga, back the fuck up off my woman," I joked.

"I done told you bout that fuckin mouth Gotti; you ain't too old for me to knock you the fuck out," he threatened.

"Punks jump up to get beat down, you better ask about me, LB." I laughed.

My mom just shook her head, while Azuri looked on in shock.

"Cut it out you two! Don't mind them baby, both of these niggas crazy." She laughed.

She told Azuri to come into the kitchen with her, so I kissed her lips and sent her on her way before sitting down next to my pops.

"She a good look for you, son." He nodded.

"Yea, that's my baby right there, man." I smiled.

"Ah shit, yo ass done fucked around and fell in love, all over here googly eyed and shit." He laughed.

"Fuck outta here." I laughed.

"But seriously, she's the one for you; I can sense that shit. She's beautiful, smart, well-mannered, and I can tell that she's loyal. Don't make the same mistakes I made wit your mother, cause I almost lost her, but I'm glad I didn't. A piece of pussy ain't worth comin in between what you got with the right one."

"Listen at you tryin to drop knowledge and shit," I smirked. "But I feel what you sayin, pops; Azuri is a good girl and I just want to make her happy."

"Then do that son and she'll be down for you harder than any of them niggas on the streets will. Believe me, I learned that shit the hard way. I know it's easy to cheat and shit, especially with these sack chasers throwin it out there at you. But before you do some fucked up shit, ask yourself if it's worth it."

I nodded my head, letting him know that I heard everything he was saying. I appreciated the talks like this I had with my pops; he had been in my shoes, so I took a lot of what he said to heart.

Jahzir and Megan showed up a little while later; I was glad that her and Azuri hit it off. My baby needed some fucking friends, cause I hadn't seen her with anybody besides Naomi hoe ass since I met her.

Dinner went off without a hitch and everybody liked Azuri, which was good shit. I watched her most of the night as she smiled and talked with my fam. She was damn near perfect and even though I knew I would eventually fuck up, I would do everything in my power to keep her happy.

Maybe pops was right earlier; maybe I was falling in love with her little ass and I didn't mind not one bit.

Chapter 15: Azuri

Everything between Kashmir, or should I say Kashy, and I was going good up until the point I met his family. It wasn't that I didn't like his family. They all welcomed me with opened arms and I loved that. What I didn't care too much for was his mother offering me a job. I was grateful that she wanted me to work with her but I had this feeling it was because of Kashmir. I knew me working at McDonald's wasn't the ideal job but at the end of the day, that was my job. I didn't need nor want any handouts. If he was going to be with me, that meant accepting all of me, including my job. I was off today, so I was supposed to go over to his house after I finished running errands.

I walked into Payomatic to pay the rent for the month and a smile quickly spread across my face. It was empty as hell and I couldn't have been any happier. I walked right up to the counter, letting the lady know I wanted to pay my rent.

"I'm sorry but there is a notice on your account saying that it has been paid off for the year," she said, passing me back my money and rent slip.

"No, there must be a mistake. Can you double check for me?"

"I'm sure there is no mistake but I will double check." I waited a couple of seconds for her to tell me that there was indeed a mistake, but she never said those words.

"Like I said before, there is a notice saying that it has been paid up for a year."

"Uh okay, thank you." I headed out of the check cashing place, pulling my phone out of my pocket. Kashmir was the first person I called because this had his name written all over it.

"Wassup Zuri, you finished handling yo business?"

"Did you pay my rent up for a year?" I asked, getting right to the point.

"Chill out with that attitude shit. So what if I did?"

"What do you mean so what if you did, Gotti? My rent and my job have nothing to do with you. I can pay my rent without your help and if I want another job, then I would go out and find one. Which I haven't, so that should tell you something."

"What the fuck should it tell me that you like smelling like fried food and shit? You over here buggin bout something that these other chicks would be sucking my dick for."

No the fuck he didn't say that shit. He got me all the way fucked up, I thought to myself. "You think I give a fuck what these other bitches would do because news flash muthafucker, I don't. I don't give a flying fuck 'bout what these bitches is out here sucking dick for. All I know is that you are overstepping your boundaries and I don't appreciate that shit at all."

"Are you my girl?"

"That has nothing to do with what we are talking about right now."

"It has everything to do with what the fuck we talkin about. Are you my girl? Yes or fucking no, Azuri."

"Yeah, I guess I am."

"Then that means there are no fucking boundaries ma. All I did was try to help you, nothing more and nothing less. Instead of bitchin', you might want to thank a nigga."

"You was trying to help me but I didn't ask for your help. I'm not one of these girls out here that's looking for a hustla or a baller to help her out. I'm not looking for a come up. I can handle this shit on my own. I was doing it before I met you and guess what? I'm going to continue to do it while I'm with you. But what I will not do is allow you to act like you're god's gift to us women. I will not tolerate you acting as if you did me a favor and now I have to kiss your ass. This whole cocky nigga persona you got going on impresses these cum buckets in the streets. It does nothing for me. The person I have been dating for the past two months is Kashmir. I might have met Gotti, but Kashy is the person that I thought I was building something with. Don't let this street shit cause you to lose me." And with that, I hung up the phone.

Deep down, I knew that Kashmir was trying to help me but I wished he would've talked to me about it first. Communication was the biggest thing to me and, without it, I felt like we had nothing. What made matters worse was the fact Kashmir tried to make it seem like I should be on my knees thanking him for what he did. That shit right there hurt me because that wasn't him. I didn't know much about what he did in the streets but, from the way Naomi talked, he was ruthless and didn't give a fuck. I have never witnessed that side of him, which was why I never called him Gotti unless I was mad. Kashmir was always attentive and caring when he was around me. Even though he still said slick shit when he was around me, for the most part we were good together. We played around like Martin and Gina. I was really starting to let my guard down with this nigga but after that shit he just said, I was pulling that shit right back up.

* * * *

Instead of going to Kashmir's house like I planned to, I decided to go chill with my cousin. I would've called up Megan but I didn't want to bother her with my drama. She was cool and everything; I just wasn't use to being around females. When I called Naomi, she was downtown in Brooklyn shopping. I told her I would catch a cab over there because I wasn't in the mood to take the train. Plus, thanks to Kashmir, I had extra money in my pocket. Pulling up to Macy's, I caught Naomi walking out the door with some chick I didn't recognize.

"You done shopping?" I asked Naomi. I wanted to go out and get something to eat because I was starving.

"I want to go into House of Hoops real quick and cop me those new Huaraches that dropped."

"Okay, then, let's go. I wanna buy me some new kicks too," I told her.

"What do you know about Dru?" Naomi asked.

"Dru who?"

"Gotti's boy, Dru," she said, sucking her teeth as if I was supposed to know that.

"I don't know nothing about him. Kashmir doesn't really talk about that street stuff with me and his brother is the only person I met, besides his family."

"Oh bitch, you met the family," Naomi said while smiling.

"Yeah, I met them a couple of days ago. They all cool."

"You lucked up when you got with Gotti. If I was you, I wouldn't even be working at McDonald's anymore."

"Just because my man has money doesn't mean I'm going to stop making mine. I love you, Naomi, but you have to get out of this hoe mentality," I sighed.

"What do you mean hoe mentality?" she snapped.

"I'm not trying to offend you; what I'm trying to say is instead of looking for guys who have something to offer you, why don't you work on having something to offer them. You are a beautiful girl, there is no denying that, but just because you have it doesn't mean you have to flaunt it. Sometimes, less is more boo." I loved my cousin and if she wasn't so out there. then we probably would be closer than what we are.

"I understand what you're saying," was all she said, bringing the conversation to the end.

As we were heading into House of Hoop, a chick was walking out and she bumped me out of nowhere. I knew it was on purpose because she had more than enough room to walk out without touching me.

"I'm going to let you pass since that bump was nothing but a love tap," I told her before turning around.

"Bitch, love tap my ass. You know what it is, which is why yo punk ass ain't doing shit," the girl spat.

I stopped in my tracks and looked over my shoulder; the bitch had come back in the store. I wasn't the type for drama but I didn't play disrespect either. I let her ass think I was going to ignore her and walked over to where Naomi was.

"I'm 'bout to go beat this bitch ass, hurry up and get your sneakers so we can be out once I finish."

"Wait, what bitch?" she asked, walking around the store.

"The chick running her mouth at the front of the store," I told her. I didn't know who this chick was but she was going on and on 'bout how I was a punk bitch.

"Girl, you don't know who that is?" Naomi asked.

"No and I don't really care, either."

"That's Zena, she used to mess with Gotti." As soon as Naomi said the name, I realized who she was. That was the chick Kashmir brought up to my job that night he picked me up. I now understood why this bitch was running her mouth crazy.

"Well, hurry up. I'll be outside," I told her and walked towards the girl.

I smirked at her as I walked past and went outside. Just like I knew she would, she followed me out the door still ranting and raving.

"You some punk bitch. I'll be damn if I let some chick talk this much shit to me and I not say anything back." She laughed.

"You talking all that shit but I have yet to see you do anything besides talk shit. Why are you so mad, lil mama?" I asked.

"Bitch, you got nerve, talkin bout why am I so mad. Mad about what? Nah, matter a fact, I am mad. I'm mad at the fact Gotti chose to fuck with yo raggedy French fry minimum wage making ass. You must be his latest charity case. Trust, when he gets done helping the needy, he will be right back to where he belongs, which is in between my legs." For emphasis, this bitch patted her pussy, as if it was on fire.

I laughed because now we were getting down to the issue. "If I was you, I wouldn't be out here patting like that; someone might think you got something." A small crowd formed around because of Zena's loud mouth.

"Me, a charity case, never. I get my own bread and pay my own bills. You, on the other hand, must be one of the bitches that sucks his dick for rent money. You out here showing yo ass because a bitch that works in McDonald's pulled the nigga of yo dreams. You out here looking real pitiful over a nigga that could care less 'bout yo dusty ass. You know what? I'm not even going to put my hands on you like I started to because I understand why you're mad. Trust me, baby girl, I do. If I was yo troll looking ass who could only get a nigga to come around when he wanted some sloppy toppy, I would be mad and hurt too."

I started laughing as Naomi walked out of the store and over to where I was standing. Before I knew it, this bitch lunged on me, knocking me to the ground. She snuffed me in the face a couple of times but that was nothing. Naomi pulled her off of me by her hair and I was able to get up. Once I was on my feet, it was murder she wrote. I pushed Naomi out of the way because I didn't want people thinking we were jumping the bitch. I hit Zena with a right jab and then a left hook. I was giving her ass the business when I heard sirens in the distance.

I let Zena go, and Naomi and I took off running. We got around the corner and jumped in her car, out of breath.

"Azuri, you fucked that girl up but you didn't have to push me like that," Naomi said, once her breathing was under control.

"Yes the fuck I did because you were getting in all the hits." I laughed.

"We may not be close but you're still my family and I wasn't going to let no bitch over step." I nodded my head because her actions proved her words to be true.

Naomi drove off and my phone began ringing. I looked down and saw that it was Kashmir. I wasn't in the mood to talk to him, so I sent his ass straight to voicemail. Not even a second later, a text came through

Kashy:

Get 2 my fuckin' house now!!

I rolled my eyes at the text and slipped my phone back in my bag.

"Where do you want to go? You still want to get something to eat? Naomi asked.

"Yeah, I guess we can go to Wing Stop since we not too far from there anyway," I told her.

She made a quick U-turn and headed in the direction of Wing Stop. Kashmir thought because he told me to do something, I was just supposed to jump. He was in the wrong and I was going to teach him a lesson. I wasn't these bitches in the street; he wasn't going to have me fall in line. I would head to Kashmir's house when I was good and damn well ready, which wasn't any time soon.

Chapter 16: Gotti

I swear me and Azuri just couldn't fuckin get right, if it wasn't one thing it was another. I knew her little ass was gon be pissed, but shit, a nigga was just trying to lighten the load a lil bit for her. All she did was fuckin work, so I figured if I paid her bills up for a year, she would have more time for me.

Maybe I could've talked to her about it, but that wasn't how I rolled; I just did shit. I knew I shouldn't have said the shit I said to her, but shit, all I knew how to do was speak facts.

Pacing the floor, I waited for her to arrive after I sent her the text. I already knew what went down outside of House of Hoops because I had eyes and ears everywhere. If that wasn't bad enough, somebody had recorded the shit and put it on the internet. I was stunned to see her working Zena's ass over like that; my baby was straight raw wit it.

After waiting for Azuri for a whole hour, I realized she wasn't coming, so I was going to find her little ass. She could be mad all she wanted. I didn't give a fuck about that, but I wasn't gon stand for her iggin my ass. Rushing out the house, I hopped in the whip and peeled out.

She must've put my ass on the block list, cause my calls were now going straight to voicemail. That pissed me off even more. I bit my bottom lip harder with each call that went to the voicemail.

Turning on Fulton St., I spotted her and Naomi's trick ass coming out of Wing Stop. Immediately spotting Naomi's car, I sped up and illegally parked so that she couldn't move it. Jumping out my whip, I walked full speed to Azuri.

"This what the fuck you on?" I asked, getting in her face.

"Get the fuck out of my face wit that bullshit Gotti!" she spat.

"What I tell you about that shit? What's my name, Azuri?" I asked her through clenched teeth.

"Shit, I don't fuckin know, who are you today? Cause the muthafucka that went and paid my rent up without talkin to me has to be Gotti. That's the nigga that got bitches on deck, right? That's the nigga that does what the fuck he wants, right? Fuck outta here my nigga," she said angrily, trying to side step me.

I grabbed her arm and pulled her into me.

"Aye, chill the fuck out man!" I shouted when she tried to pull away.

"Let me go Kashmir," she sighed.

"No, we bout to go talk about this shit," I told her.

"I'm not goin nowhere wit you!"

"Yes the fuck you are! Now, either we can do this shit the easy way or I can embarrass yo muthafuckin ass out here; the choice is yours."

She stared at me evilly and I stared right back at her little ass; she wasn't scaring shit over here anyway. Sucking her teeth, she turned her attention back to Naomi.

"You can go head, I'll call you later," she told her.

Naomi laughed and shook her head before walking off toward her car. Azuri stomped angrily to my truck and hopped in, slamming the fuck outta my door. I counted to ten in my head before following her simple ass.

"Don't slam my fuckin door like that no more," I spat before pulling off.

She igged my ass and buried her face in her phone. That shit pissed me off, so I snatched it out her hand and threw it out the window.

"Why the fuck would you do that stupid shit?!" she shouted.

"Cause, you always got yo fuckin face in that muthafucka when I'm tryin to talk to yo simple ass!"

"I swear I can't fuckin stand you!"

I igged her ass and turned the radio up, heading to my house so we could talk.

As soon as we pulled up, she hopped out and speed walked to the door. She had a key, so she walked in and closed the door damn near in my face. I was two seconds from snapping on her ass, so I walked back to my truck and grabbed a pre-rolled blunt.

Sparking it up, I made my way back to the house and sat down on the front steps to smoke. I sat out there and faced the whole blunt before making my way inside. I didn't have to look for her to know where she was. I had a huge bay window in my room with a bench attached to it.

Whenever Azuri got pissed, she would go over to that little area, put in her headphones, and zone out. Entering my room, I rounded the corner and, just as I thought, she was sitting there with her head leaned up against the window and her eyes closed.

I just stared at her for a little while. Azuri wasn't only beautiful on the outside, but so was her heart. Yea, I was wrong for how I went about shit, but I just wanted to take care of her; was that so wrong? This girl had my head gone, there wasn't nothing in this world that I wouldn't do for her.

"Why are you staring at me?" she asked, snapping me out of my thoughts.

"Damn, a nigga can't look at you, ma?" I asked her.

"Whatever Kashmir, I'm not about to argue with you," she replied, while sighing.

"Come on ma, we need to talk," I said, approaching her.

She sucked her teeth as I pulled her up and led her to my bed. I sat her down on top of me and scooted toward the headboard.

"Tell me what's on your mind," I told her, while looking into her eyes.

"I know that you have money Kashy, but that's not why I'm with you. I'm with you because I just want you. I don't need the perks and all that other shit, just you. It's not that I don't appreciate what you did, it's just that I don't like feeling like anybody's charity case."

"That's not why I did it ma. I did it because I see how hard you work and I wanted to be able to lighten the load a little bit.

Azuri, you're only twenty-one and all you do is work. I'm not knocking that because I respect that, but you still gotta live, ma. Maybe I should've talked to you about it, so for that I apologize, but never ever feel like anything I do for you is charity."

"I get that Kashy, I really do, but you have to understand that this is what I've been doing since high school. I'm not used to anybody helping me, so when you did that without talking to me, it pissed me off. Not only that, but I know you had something to do with your mother offering me a job," she said.

"Yea I did, but that's only because I want more for you than Mickey D's. Yea, I know that's your hustle, but ain't you tired of that shit? I mean, you work like a slave for a little more than minimum wage; you're better than that shit, ma. So yea, I asked my dukes if there was anything you could do at her store and it just so happened that she just fired her manager. If you want the job, then it's yours, but if you don't, then that's all good too," I told her.

"I just want the best for you, ma, and I want you to be happy. I know you got goals and shit, so I'm just tryin to do whatever I can to help you achieve them. Workin for my dukes puts more money in your pocket and you'll be able to set your own schedule; that way you can go back to school and shit," I added.

"Wow, I never knew you felt like that Kashy; I just assumed that you wanted to control me and wanted me to depend on you." She shrugged.

"Never that ma, I would never ask you to depend on me; nothing is sexier than a woman that knows how to get out here and get her own." I winked, causing her to blush.

"Ok, I'll take the job." She smiled.

I nodded my head and grinned at her before leaning in to kiss her lips. She sucked gently on my bottom lip, causing my dick to wake up.

"You better stop that shit girl; a nigga ain't had no pussy in a few months," I told her seriously.

"Then maybe we need to change that," she smirked before pulling her shirt over her head.

"You sure?" I asked her.

"I'm sure," she replied.

That was all I needed to hear before capturing her bottom lip in my mouth and sticking my tongue down her throat. My hands found their way to her breasts, massaging them gently and causing her to moan in my mouth. Expertly unhooking her bra, I took her Hershey kiss sized nipples into my mouth and sucked on them.

"Mmmm…" she moaned, throwing her head back.

After showing her breasts equal attention, I laid her on her back, helping her out of her pants and underwear. Pulling my shirt over my head, I got down eye level with her peach and dove in head first.

"Ohhhh damnnnn baby!" she cried out.

Slipping a finger inside of her, I wrapped my lips around her bud and sucked it like I had done her nipples a little while ago. I nibbled gently while moving my finger in and out of her, causing her to damn near come off the bed. For the next thirty minutes, I drowned myself in her juices, bringing her to back to back orgasms.

"You good ma?" I asked, smirking as I wiped her juices from my face.

She panted heavily with her eyes halfway opened, giving me a lazy grin before nodding. Pulling my pants off, she took me by surprise when she crawled over to me and took my dick in her mouth.

"Fuck!" I groaned as she took me down her throat.

She jerked my dick and spat on it before taking me back into her mouth again. My toes dug into the carpet and my eyes rolled up in my head. Azuri was giving me some of the best sloppy toppy I had ever experienced.

Popping my dick out her mouth, she dipped her head lower and started sucking my balls while she jacked my dick. I had to push her little ass back cause I was on the verge of cumming.

"What's wrong?" she asked.

"I was bout to cum," I replied honestly.

She smirked lightly and blushed a little, no doubt giving herself props in her head.

"Turn around," I ordered.

Doing as she was told, she wiggled her ass a little, making her butt cheeks claps. I slid into her slowly and a nigga almost came; her shit was like a vice grip pulling me in.

"Uhhhh..." she moaned.

I bit my bottom lip to keep from crying out like a bitch and smacked her ass when she started throwing it back. Grabbing her waist, I halted her movements and went in deeper, hitting her spot with each stroke. She tried to run, but I held her little ass in place.

"The fuck you think you going," I asked her huskily.

"Ahhhh shit, I'm gonna cum baby!" she screamed.

"Let that shit go then," I ordered and she did just that.

She had my dick looking like I had stuck it in a vanilla milkshake when she came. Pulling out of her, I turned her over and climbed back inside, kissing her passionately. She wrapped her legs around my waist and pulled me in deeper, causing both of us to moan.

I looked at her and she looked back at me with tears in her eyes.

"You ok ma?" I asked, slowing up my strokes.

"I'm ok baby, I'm just riding the wave," she said softly.

Burying my face into her neck, she wrapped her arms around my neck as she fucked me from the bottom. Grinding into her, she clamped her muscles around my dick and squeezed. I felt my nut coming and sped up a little bit.

"Cum wit me ma," I groaned, kissing her lips.

Moments later, we were both cumming and I was filling her up with buckets of cum. A nigga was spent and I just collapsed on top of her, both of us breathing heavily.

Pulling out of her, I fell on my back and pulled her close to me.

"Damn, I love you, girl," I mumbled.

"What did you just say?" she asked, sitting up slightly to look at me.

"I said I love you, ma. I ain't never told no other woman that except my mother. You fucked around and got a nigga on stuck, especially after feeling the softest place on earth; you stuck wit my black ass now," I said, patting her kitty.

"You so damn silly." She giggled. "I love you too, Kashmir," she said softly.

"I know you do ma, I know you do," I told her.

We snuggled up closer together, too tired to get up and shower. It wasn't long before sleep found us and a nigga went to sleep with a smile on his face.

Chapter 17: Azuri

Between the sun shining in my face and Kashy's loud snoring, I didn't know which one was annoying me more. I yawned and stretched a little before unraveling myself from Kashmir's arms.

"Where you going ma?" he asked sleepily

"You are snoring too loud, so I'm about to get up and get my day started."

"Lay yo ass back down. It's not like you have to go to work, chill with me for the day." He went to pull me back in bed but I dodged his grasp.

"We can spend the day together; I just don't want to make it a habit of me sleeping late into the day. I still have to go to my old job and give them my two-week notice."

"I don't want you workin there for another two weeks ma. My moms need you to start asap."

"I understand that but I'm not going to leave on a bad note. You never know what can happen, I may need that job back or something," I explained.

"Nah, I doubt that shit cause even if we don't work out, the manager job will always be yours," he told me and I believed him too.

"Okay, well I'm going to take your Camaro. It's ten now, so I should be back by one, then we can spend the rest of the day together."

"Iight ma, be good."

"I'm always good." I giggled.

I gave him a soft kiss before throwing a pillow at his face. I rushed out the room before he could get up and try to attack me. I grabbed my overnight bag that I packed and left in his living room, then took off for the bathroom. After showering, lotioning my body, and getting dressed, I was ready to head out the door. I grabbed

Kashmir's key ring and took off the keys for his Camaro. I was about to walk out the door when his voice stopped me in my tracks

"Where the fuck you think you going in those short ass shorts?"

It was early June but summer didn't take its time getting here. I checked the weather app on Kashy's phone and it was supposed to be ninety degrees out today. The shorts I had on were short, but they weren't that short.

"I'm going to put in my two-week notice. I already told you that." I smiled.

"Don't play games with me, Zuri. Go change your clothes. The fuck you thought this was."

"Kashy, you're overreacting; my shorts are not even that short. See." I turned around, so he could see that my whole ass was covered. "My butt isn't even hanging out."

"That's cause you barely have an ass. Now, go change them damn shorts and stop with the whining. Matter of fact, I'm about to roll with you."

"No, Kashmir, I'll change my clothes but I don't want you coming with me."

"Why not? You got something to hide or are you going to see your other nigga?"

"There is no other nigga. I just wanted to hurry up and get this over with but if you must come, then hurry up."

"Yeah iight, there better not be no other nigga. I'll fuck yo little ass up and send that nigga to an early grave."

"Whatever Gotti." I rolled my eyes because he was being annoying as hell.

"Gotti these nuts, go change," he said, then walked away.

I picked up my overnight bag and looked through it for something else to wear. I took out a pair of joggers and a sports bra. I changed my clothes right there in the living room, then sat on the couch waiting for Kashmir to finish getting ready. I went to pull out my phone, then remembered this nigga threw it out the window. He didn't know it yet, but he was about to upgrade my shit. I had the iPhone 4s, but I had my eye on the iPhone 6 Plus. It was only right that Kashmir got me a new one.

Ten minutes turned into twenty and twenty turned into thirty. Before I knew it, a whole hour passed and Kashmir still hadn't come back to the living room. I hopped off the couch and went to go find him because I was ready to go.

"Kashmir, come on. I want to get this over with." I stormed in the bedroom.

"Calm your little ass down; I'm coming now. You look cute ma," he said, eyeing me.

"I looked cute before too but you know how yo controlling ass is." I giggled.

"I'm not trying to control you, ma. I'm just trying not to catch a body today. You too fine to leave behind."

"Oh, shut up with your corny ass. Don't forget your ass is buying me a new phone." I laughed.

"Yeah whatever, come one, let's go."

He grabbed his things off the dresser, then wrapped his arms around my waist and led me out the room. We got outside and I threw my overnight bag in the back seat. I got in and pulled off with my nigga riding shot gun. During the ride, I would steal glances at him. Kashmir was an asshole but he was my asshole. It was weird but we brought out the best and the worse out of each other. I could tell our relationship wasn't going to be easy, but I would weather the storm as long as I could have him at the end of every day.

* * * *

"Where you want to go now?" I asked him. I handed in my two-week notice and my manager said it was unnecessary for me to work the extra two weeks. I was happy about that because I honestly didn't want to go back. After leaving McDonald's we headed to the nearest T-Mobile to get my new iPhone.

"It's up to you, Zuri. It's your world; I'm just trying to be in it."

"Let's go to the Rucker. I wanna ball," I told him.

"You sure that's what you want to do?" he asked, sounding skeptical.

"Yeah." I smiled. "I haven't played in a while and I really miss it."

"Iight then that's where we headed. You wanna go to the crib and grab you something else to wear?"

"Nah, I'm good. I can ball in this. I do need to go home and check on my mother. I would've called her this morning but you know someone threw my phone out the window."

"I'll get you a new one, don't even trip. Yeah, let's go see mama dukes real quick."

"Mama dukes, really?" I laughed.

"Yeah. Just drive with your big ass head." He laughed.

I rolled my eyes at him because he was so fucking goofy when he wanted to be. Pulling up in front of my building, Kashmir got out and said wassup to a couple of people that he knew. I used my key to unlock the door; I left the door slightly opened for Kashy.

"Ma!" I called out.

"Why are you yelling girl? And why didn't you call me to let me know you weren't coming home last night? I don't care how old you are Azuri, you need to check in. I worry about you," my mother said.

"I'm sorry about that Nala. She couldn't call because I allowed my anger to get the best of me and I threw her phone out the window," Kashmir said, walking in the door.

"That is still no excuse. It's nice seeing you again Kashmir." My mother smiled.

She moved around me and walked over to him just to give him a hug. I was glad my mother and Kashmir got along because if she didn't like him, then there would be no us.

"What do you young folks have planned for the day?" she asked, sitting on the couch.

"Zuri think she can take me in ball. We 'bout to go up to the Rucker and shoot some hoops," Kashmir told her.

"I haven't been to the Rucker in years," My mother said.

"You should come with us. You can wipe the tears from your daughter's eyes when I show her who's boss."

"Uh no, she cannot. You know how they are out there and I don't need my mother getting caught up," I said.

"Chill out Azuri; the both of you are going to be with me. Niggas know not to act funny in my presence, it will be fine. Nala, go get dressed and you can roll with us."

I ice grilled Kashmir as my mother got up and went back towards her room.

"You can stop looking at me like that and come give me a kiss."

"I'm not kissing you because you don't listen. I told you I don't want my mother out there."

"Azuri, your mother may have an illness but she's not a couch potato. You can't keep her stuck up in the house all because you are afraid of what may happen. Just like you need to get out and have some fun, so does she." He walked closer to me and wrapped my arms around his neck. "I got you, Azuri, and that means I got yo mother as well. I promise you, nothing is going to happen to you or your mother as long as I'm around. I love you, ma." He cupped my chin and tilted my head up towards him.

"I love you, too," I whispered back.

He leaned down and kissed me and I melted into the kiss. I trusted Kashmir but this was my mother we were talking about. My mother was my heart and if anything happened to her, I would be crushed.

Chapter 18: Gotti

"I told you I'm nice," Azuri smirked before crossing me up and laying the ball up.

I sucked my teeth at her and shook my head. I ain't gon front though, her handles was nice, but ain't no way in hell she was bout to beat me. We were running a game of twenty-one while Nala looked on. The current score was tied at eighteen.

"Check!" she said, throwing me the ball.

I let that shit bounce off my chest like ol buddy did in *Love and Basketball*, then hit her ass with a smirk. Paying close attention to her, I noticed that she dribbled on the right and crossed on the left. Guarding her closely, I waited for the right time to strike and stole the ball from her ass.

She huffed in frustration and I grinned, before pulling up and draining a mean ass jumper in her face.

I could tell she was pissed by the stank ass look on her face. She checked the ball again and I didn't even move; I just pulled up and drained another jumper.

"One and done baby," I said, blowing her a kiss.

She looked at me evilly and rolled them big ass eyes super hard; that shit was amusing to me cause she was really mad.

"How you want it this time baby?" I asked her, as I dribbled the ball through my legs.

"Just shut up Kashmir and play," she said through clenched teeth.

Nodding my head, I dribbled the ball a few more times as she guarded me tightly, then I hit her ass wit a crossover that Allen Iverson would be proud of, before dunking the ball.

"That's game," I smirked.

She stomped off toward the bleachers and snatched her water up, guzzling it down with attitude.

"You see how I did your daughter dirty ma?" I asked Nala, as she was approaching.

"Oh hush up, she was bout to take it to yo ass," she said laughing.

"Rematch?" I asked Azuri.

"Maybe another day." She shrugged.

Before I could respond, gunshots rang out, causing me to pull Azuri and Nala to the ground. I shielded them from the gunfire as best I could, cursing myself for leaving my gun in the car.

My blood boiled with each bullet that was released. It was more than just us at the park, so I couldn't say for sure if they were shooting at me or not. At this point, that shit didn't even matter though. My girl and her mother were out here, along with a bunch of fuckin kids, so for that alone, I was coming for whoever it was.

Moments later, the gunfire ceased and I slowly peeled myself away from them.

"Y'all good?" I asked them.

"Yea, I'm good, you ok mommy?" Azuri asked.

No response.

"Mom?" Azuri cried, shaking Nala.

"Aw fuck!" I said to myself, watching the blood pour from the hole in her shoulder.

Kneeling down beside her, I felt for a pulse and it was still there. Azuri was crying hard as hell, while I checked to see if the bullet went through and it did.

"Azuri!" I said, grabbing her shoulders to calm her down. "I need you to calm down; she was just hit in the shoulder and it went through. Her pulse is still strong, we just gotta get her to a hospital."

She nodded her head, grabbing the keys out my bag. Carefully picking Nala up, I walked her to my truck and laid her in the back. Azuri climbed in beside her, placing her head gently on her lap. I peeled out of the parking lot and headed for Bellevue Hospital.

Ten minutes later, we were pulling up. I illegally parked and ran inside. A few seconds later, I was running back out with nurses in tow, pushing a gurney.

They pulled Nala out, cut her shirt away, and rushed her inside.

"Female gunshot victim, a lot of blood loss, current state unconscious, let's move people!" the doctor shouted, as we rushed in behind them.

They pushed her in the back and a nurse directed us to the waiting room. I pulled Azuri onto my lap and hugged her tightly as she cried.

"I can't lose her. If I lose her, I won't survive; she's all I have," she said softly with tears falling down her face.

"She gon be good ma," I assured her.

We sat in silence for a little while, then she jumped up and turned to me with an evil glare.

"This is all your fault! I told you I didn't want my mother at the Rucker, but you just had to insist and look what happened! Those niggas were probably shooting at you anyway and my mother got caught up in the crossfire! You said you would protect me and look what happened Kashmir! Being with you almost cost me my mother," she said, shaking her head.

"So, what you saying Zuri?" I asked, grilling her.

"I'm... I'm sayin that being with you is dangerous, somebody was gunning for you and my mother was shot!"

"Gunning for me? How you know, huh? It was other muthafuckas at the park, but you blaming me? I protected you two the best that I could, but shit happens, that's life. You wanna blame me, then fine, do whatever the fuck makes you happy. I don't know who the fuck those niggas was gunning for, but I'll get down to the bottom of it. I love you, Azuri, but if you don't trust me to keep you safe, then what the fuck we together for?"

"Maybe we shouldn't be," she said softly.

I took a step back and eyed her to see if she was serious; her face held a blank expression. Before saying some shit that I would regret, I nodded my head, kissed her forehead, and walked toward the door.

"I love you Azuri, that's some real shit. But, like you said, being with me is dangerous, right? I'll protect you at any cost, even if it means letting you go," I told her before walking out.

This shit had my head fucked up, to know that she blamed a nigga hurt. Shit, I would do anything for Azuri and her mom; hell, I would've gladly took that bullet for Nala, but shit didn't happen like that.

Hopping in my truck, I headed home, facing a blunt the entire way. The shit Azuri said to me had my ass gone; the look in her eyes told me she meant that shit.

Pulling up to the crib, I sighed heavily before climbing out and heading inside. Stripping out of my bloody clothes, I tossed them in a bag and stepped into the hot shower. Placing my hands on the wall in front of me, I dropped my head and let the water run over my head.

I meant what I said to Azuri; if she didn't trust me enough to keep her safe, then what the fuck was the point of us being together? Thirty minutes later, I was getting out the shower and wrapping a towel around my waist.

Azuri ran through my mind heavily and I wanted nothing more than to take my ass back up to the hospital, pull her into my arms, and hold her tight. I loved her little ass, but I couldn't be with her right now. First things first, I had to get down to the bottom of who shot up the Rucker.

"Yo!" Jahzir answered.

"Where you?"

"Shit, heading to the crib, what's up?"

"Come through, I need to holla at you about something," I told him.

"No doubt, be there in ten," he said before hanging up.

Throwing on an all-black sweat suit, I rolled a blunt while I waited on Jahzir. I had love for my niggas, but Jahzir was the only one I really trusted like that. He was my blood and I knew he would have my back through whatever.

"What's happenin bruh?" he asked, walking through the door.

"Somebody shot at me today," I told him, while lighting the blunt.

"The fuck you mean somebody shot at you today?" he asked angrily.

"Just what the fuck I said," I replied, passing him the blunt.

I quickly ran down the full story and, by the time I was done, this nigga was ready to go to war. Sometimes, I forgot this nigga was the little brother and I was the big brother.

"So, Azuri's mom straight?" he asked, once he calmed down.

"I couldn't tell you." I shrugged.

"The fuck that supposed to mean?"

"She flipped out on a nigga man, started blaming me and shit, so instead of saying some shit I would regret, I just left," I told him.

"Man, that girl ain't mean none of that shit; she runnin off emotions and she's hurt, so she had to blame somebody. You were the only one there, so naturally she took her anger out on you," he explained.

"Nah bruh, she meant that shit; I saw it in her eyes. It is what it is though." I shrugged.

I was trying to act like this shit wasn't fazing me, but it was. Azuri was my heart, so without her, a nigga felt dead inside. Shaking my head, I chuckled to myself; she had my ass gone off her little ass.

"Man, that girl loves you and you love her, this shit right here is just a test of y'all relationship. Either you gon stick it out with her or you gon let her go, simple as that. Some shit is worth fighting for Kash," he told me.

"I hear you, Dr. Phil," I chuckled.

"I'm just speakin some real shit, you remember the shit I went through with Megan."

I nodded my head, remembering the test that his relationship with Megan went through. A few years ago, her brother was killed. He was working for us at the time, but cutting side deals that we didn't know about. One night, he went to meet up with some niggas and never made it back home. Megan spazzed out on both of our asses and cussed Jahzir out something terrible.

They went through a bad rough patch in their relationship, but my brother never gave up on her and ultimately they got back together.

"I'm gon give her some space right now, so I can get down to the bottom of this shit," I told him.

"Well, I texted Megan and told her what happened; she's on her way up there now," he replied.

I nodded my head, glad that Azuri wouldn't be up there by herself.

"Let's hit these streets and find out what the fuck happened," I said, getting up and grabbing my keys.

I didn't know if these niggas were gunning for me or not, but they had violated in the worst way, so for that they had to die. I shook thoughts of Azuri out my mind and headed out the door with my brother in tow, ready to wage war on the streets of NY.

Chapter 19: Azuri

Sitting in my mom's room watching her laid up in a hospital bed kind of put everything in perspective for me. I told Kash I didn't want to bring my mother to the courts for this exact reason, but he wouldn't listen to me. He had to be right and in control with everything or he wasn't going for it. I couldn't be with a man like him because he didn't listen. He simply did what he wanted to, while everyone else dealt with repercussions.

"Hey, Jahzir told me you were here, how is she doing?" Megan asked, walking into the room.

"She's fine. The doctor said the bullet went right through, they want her to stay overnight to monitor her. I guess they want to make sure that everything is under control with her Lupus. I know you're here to check on me, but I would love to be alone right now."

"Azuri, stop trying to always be strong; it's okay to cry on someone's shoulder or just to let your feelings out. Even the strongest people break down every once in a while. You may not want to talk but I'm not leaving," Megan said.

"Thanks," I whispered as the tears began to fall. She was right; I was always the one that had to be strong, even when I didn't think I had the strength.

"Oh no, don't cry Zuri. Talk to me," she said, passing me some tissues.

"I don't even know where to begin. My mom is laid up in the hospital and Kashmir and I can't seem to get it right."

"Well, when it comes to your mother, I don't know her but I do know she is a strong woman, especially because she raised you to be a strong woman. Yes, your mother has an illness, but you can't treat her like an invalid. You have to let your mother live her life just like you have to live yours. Now, her getting shot is sad but the doctor said she's going to be okay, so stop beating yourself up behind that."

"You just don't understand. My mother is all I have; if I lose her then I would have nobody."

"That's not true; you will have me, but you will also have Gotti."

"No I won't, I broke up with him," I told her. Saying the words out loud brought a slight pain to my heart. I wasn't sure if breaking up with Kashy was what I wanted, but it seemed like the right thing to do.

"You think because you broke up with him he's going to leave you alone? Girl please, give that man a couple of days or a week tops and he will be right back sniffing up under you."

"I doubt it. I blamed him for my mother getting shot. I told him the dudes were gunning for him."

"Azuri, I'm about to teach you a lesson so make sure you pay attention. You live in the hood, so I don't have to tell you bullets don't have names on them. Gotti is into that street life and you knew that from the jump. He didn't lead you on, believing he did something different; he kept it real with you. He let you into his world with hopes you would be the one to tough shit out with him. The life he lives is a tough one and, yes, people do gun for Gotti but you can't blame him for another man's actions."

"I wasn't blaming him for another man's actions." I sighed.

"You told him it was his fault your mom got shot, that's blaming him for another man's actions. Look Azuri, being with someone of Gotti's caliber isn't easy, trust me. A while back, my brother got killed. He was working for Gotti and Jahzir but his little dumb ass was doing side deals. Long story short, when I found out, I cursed both of their asses out because I felt as though they should've looked out for him. They should have been there to protect him.

Jahzir and I ended up going through a rough patch because I blamed him for something he had no control over. Eventually, we got over it, but during that time, we both said some hurtful things to each other that neither one of us meant. During that time, I learned Jahzir wasn't superman; he couldn't stop everything and he couldn't protect everyone. I had to stop expecting so much from him because he was only human, like me. I had to trust that he would never do anything intentionally to make me upset and he would do his best to make sure I didn't endure any pain.

I say all of that to say this. Azuri, you have to know that Gotti is going to do his best to protect you and the ones you love at all cost, but whenever he doesn't come through, you can't blame him. You have to trust that he did everything possible to protect both you and your mother. I would bet a grand right now; he's out there looking for the person who shot your mother. Now, you say you ended things with him and maybe that is for the best; the both of you may need sometime apart. If you and him do choose to get back together, make sure you're strong enough to handle all that comes with him," Megan told me.

"I understand."

"Well, I know you're probably tired of me lecturing you, so I'm going to leave; just think about what I said."

"I will."

I hugged her good bye before she left out and promised I would talk to her tomorrow. For the rest of the night, I sat in my mother's room watching her sleep. Sleep wasn't coming easy for me and I had a million things on my mind. Once again, I was alone in my life, having to be the strong person. I needed someone by my side, I needed him. I need Kashmir.

I picked up my phone and dialed his number. It went straight to voicemail. I thought about hanging up but decided against it.

"Kashmir, I'm sorry for what I said earlier, I know it wasn't your fault. Please, just come back to the hospital, I need you, Kashy," I whispered into the phone before hanging up.

I threw my phone against the wall and allowed my tears to flow freely. I was a mess and didn't know where to start putting myself together. For so long, being strong was all I knew but it seemed like my strong nature was stopping all the blessings that were coming into my life.

As I walked back in the room, I heard my mother whispering my name.

"I'm here ma," I said, rushing to her side.

"Stop pushing Kashmir away. This wasn't his fault."

"Wait, how do you know-" I began.

"Shhhh. I know you and I know how you get when it comes to me. Yes, I got shot but I wasn't anyone's fault, except the person who pulled the trigger."

"I just regret having you there."

"Don't regret it because I don't. Seeing you smiling and having fun with someone you care for warms my heart. Don't let what happened to me stop you from having a chance at true love. Now, come here and lay with your mama." She smiled.

I cuddled in the bed with her; she drifted back to sleep as I stayed up checking my phone every hour on the hour. What I said probably hurt Kashmir, which was why he wasn't calling me back. I just hoped this was one of those things we would be able to look back at and say it made us stronger as a unit.

Chapter 20: Gotti

For four hours, me and my brother combed the streets, trying to get info on what happened at the Rucker. Just when I was about to head back to the house, I got a call from Quest, telling me to meet him at the spot. Making an illegal U-turn, I hopped on the highway and headed to the little warehouse we had out in Staten Island.

My phone buzzed as we pulled up and I listened to the message Azuri left me. It warmed a nigga's heart to know that she needed me and wanted me there with her. But, I couldn't focus on that shit right now, so I turned my phone off and dropped it in the cup holder. Grabbing my gun, I hopped out my truck with my brother in tow.

Entering the warehouse, I saw four niggas tied up in chairs side by side.

"What's good my nigga?" Quest said, slapping it up with me.

"Shit, you called me here, so you tell me," I replied.

"Well, according to my sources, these mu'fuckas are the ones that did the hit on the Rucker. Turns out, you were the target, but I haven't found out who ordered that shit yet," Quest explained.

"Is that right?" I asked, eyeing the four dead men that sat before me.

"Anybody wanna tell me who the fuck had the balls to order a hit on Gotti?" I asked, walking around the four chairs that sat before me.

"You might as well kill me homie; I ain't no snitch," one of the dudes spat.

"Ok." I shrugged before putting a bullet in his head.

"Anybody else wanna take this secret to the grave?" I asked, stepping over the chair that toppled over.

"I ain't tellin you shit either," another said.

A bullet to the head ended his life quick.

"And then there were two," I taunted.

I eyed them both, one had a blank expression on his face, while the other one looked like he was gon shit on himself. Instead of keeping them both alive, I shot the one that I knew wasn't coming off no info.

"Looks like it's on you, homie," I said, standing in front of him with my arms folded behind my back.

Silence.

"So, you gon keep up the tough guy act huh?" I asked before shooting him in the shoulder.

"Fuck! Ok man look, Tamir put out the hit, he comin for you and he wants you dead. He didn't tell us why, but he has a huge vendetta against you; that's all I know. Please, don't kill me man, I got kids!" he cried, while breathing hard.

"Yea, well you should've thought about your kids before you came for the king," I spat with venom.

He opened his mouth to speak, but a bullet to the head silenced him forever.

"Call somebody to come clean this shit up and get me all the information you can on this fuckin Tamir. I want every piece of information you can find, down to the last thing he ate for dinner," I spat heatedly before walking out the door.

I was seeing red and I wanted nothing more than to kill this muthafucka. Yea, niggas didn't like me and I didn't give a fuck, but none had balls big enough to come for me. The fact that my girl was with me and her mother got hurt had silent rage flowing through my veins.

"Kash, I already know what's goin through your head and I'm on the same page wit you. But we gotta play this smart bruh and not act on emotions. Go see yo girl man, she needs you right now. I know she said that she doesn't, but that's bullshit, you know it and I know it."

I thought about what he said and I knew that he was right. The way I was feeling, I was liable to commit some more murders and end up in a bad ass situation. My heart told me to go see Azuri, but my mind was still on the shit she said.

"Don't let your pride fuck up a good thing," Jahzir said, as I pulled up beside his car.

He dapped me up and hopped out. I sat in my car, thinking over what he said, before heading inside to shower. After burning the clothes I had on, I showered and got redressed. Azuri's message rang loudly in my head; her voice was filled with so much hurt and regret. She said she needed me and in reality, I needed her just as bad.

She was my calm, she was my happy place, that girl was my fuckin heart and I couldn't let nothing fuck up what he had. Close to an hour later, I was on an elevator headed up to the third floor of the hospital.

Quietly entering the room, I stood in the doorway and watched her sleep peacefully next to her mother. Her tear stained puffy face let me know that she had been crying and that fucked a nigga up. As if she felt my presence, she stirred in her sleep and then her eyes met mine. Tears filled her eyes as she slowly climbed out of bed with Nala.

Slowly making her way to me, she wiped her face and I pulled her into my embrace. As soon as she made contact with me, my world was right again. No words had to be spoken, she was mine and I was hers.

"I'm sorry bae, it was just so much going on and I was angry, but I-"

"Shhhh, I know ma and I ain't gon lie, that shit fucked wit a nigga, but none of that matters right now. I need you to know that I love you with everything in me, Stink, and I'll protect you all I can. Being wit a nigga like me is dangerous and I get that, but you gotta rock wit a nigga ma. You're my calm in all this bullshit. When I'm out here in these streets, knowing that I got you waitin on me is my motivation to make it home every night. Before you, I didn't give a fuck about dying, but now I do. I want you to carry my last name, give me a bunch of babies, and ride wit a nigga through thick and thin. It's us against the world Stink, I need my baby by my side ma. I ain't shit without you," I told her.

"I love you too baby and I know that I'm difficult to deal with sometimes, but I really am trying. This put a lot of things in perspective for me and yes, I was angry, but me without you isn't gonna work. I trust you to keep me safe and I'm sorry if the things I said hurt you; it's just that this is all new to me. You're my heart too Kashy and I don't need all the material bullshit, just give me you, that's all I need," she said softly.

"You got me ma." I grinned before kissing her soft lips.

"One more thing though, Stink?" she asked with a raised eyebrow.

"Yea, you dont like it?" I asked.

"I mean, I guess." She laughed.

"Good, cause you ain't got no choice, that's yo name." I laughed, kissing her again. "You makin a nigga soft ma," I told her, shaking my head.

"So what? I like this Kashy, he's definitely different from the asshole I first me," she giggled.

"You like that nigga too, especially when I'm digging in them guts," I whispered in her ear.

She slapped my chest as her face flushed. Pulling me all the way in the room, I kissed Nala on her cheek, being careful not to wake her up, before pulling Azuri onto my lap and wrapping my arms tightly around her.

I was glad that Nala was good, plus I fixed shit with my girl. I pushed Tamir to the back of my head for the moment, but make no mistake about it, tomorrow was a brand new day and I was gon hit the ground running. For now, I was gon kick it with my leading lady and escape the bullshit, if only for one day.

Chapter 21: Azuri

My mother made sure both Kashmir and I was up early as hell getting out of the hospital. My mother wasted no time having the doctors run all the necessary test, so she could get out of there. I thought it would be best for her to stay an extra day but she wasn't having it at all.

"Y'all are moving slower than the doctors did, bring y'all asses on," my mother complained, holding the elevator for Kashmir and I.

"Mom, slow down. Why are you in a rush to go in the house anyway?" I asked her.

"I'm not going in the house; I'm going to Violet's house. I got to tell her about my war wound." Kashmir started laughing and I shot him a look, wasn't nothing funny about what my mother had just said.

"Nala, you don't have no damn war wound. You're going in the house and I'm staying the day with you."

"Chill out Stink, your mother is good; you don't have to keep her cooped up in the house. She didn't die ma, so let her live."

"Yeah Azuri, let ya mom live."

"Fine, I will drop you off at Auntie Violet's but I don't want you outside acting crazy with her. You know Naomi be messing with them crazy boys around the way; I don't need you in no mess mom."

"Kash, tell my daughter that I am the mother around here because she obviously doesn't hear me when I say it."

"Stink, let yo mom be great, iight."

"I don't like this whole double teaming thing." I fake pouted.

"You gonna let me turn that frown upside down," he smirked, leaning towards me and licking my lips.

"Kashy, my mom," I whined, putting my seat belt on.

"Girl hush, you act like I don't know about the birds and the bees. How do you think you got here?"

"Ewww." I laughed.

The whole ride to my aunt's house, Kashmir and my mom talked as if I wasn't even in the car. They were just going on and on as if they were the bestest friends in the world. In the middle of their conversation, my phone started ringing. Looking at my phone screen, I didn't recognize the number.

"Hello."

"Hey Azuri, it's Gina, Kashy's mom. How are you?"

"I'm good, how are you?" I asked back to be polite.

"I'm okay. I got your number from my son when he told me you were looking for a job. I was wondering if you could come into the shop today to start filling out your paperwork and maybe start your training."

"Yeah, that would be great; what time do you need me to come in?"

"Well, it's eleven now. If you could get here by one, that would be great."

"Okay. And thank you for the opportunity, I really appreciate it."

"No thanks needed honey. I don't mind helping young motivated females out."

"Young and motivated is exactly what I am, I'll see you at one Gina."

"Alright baby," she said and hung up the phone.

"What my mom want, Stink?" Kashmir asked

"Oh, so now you acknowledge my presence?"

"Don't be jelly baby." My mother laughed as we pulled up to my aunt's house.

"Don't worry about me being jelly; just make sure you stay out of trouble. I have to go into work today, so I won't be able to check on you until later. I will be calling your phone every chance I get."

"I know you love me Azuri but sometimes, you have to let whatever is going to happen, happen. Kashmir, I just want you to know that I don't blame you at all for what happened to me."

"I appreciate that Nala, what happened to you isn't gonna go unanswered tho."

"Do what you have to do baby; just be careful. All I ask is that you make sure you keep my daughter safe."

"You have my word," Kashmir told her.

I wouldn't let Kashmir pull off until my mother was safely in the house. Even when she got in the house, I pulled out my phone to send her a text. Kashmir saw what I was doing and snatched my phone out my hand.

"Damn Stink, let yo mama breathe and shit. You suffocating her and she not even around."

"I'm just trying to make sure that she is okay. She did just get shot, you know."

"Yeah, I know she just got shot. I was there. She straight; trust me. What my moms say to you?"

"Nothing, she wants me to come in today to fill out paperwork and do some training."

"That's cool. I want you at my crib after work."

"I can't; I have to go home with my mother."

"Then yo moms can come too. I'm just trying to be next to you, Stink."

"I'll see what I can do but I'm not making any promises."

"You coming, ain't no point in seeing what you can do. What I want is what I get."

"Oh, it's just that simple?"

"Stop acting like you ain't know." He laughed.

"You get on my nervous," I giggled.

I was glad things were back on track between Kashmir and I because he was really my calm after the storm. He was the only person besides my mother who knew the real me. Everyone else got the bitch side while he got the loving and caring side.

"Getcho head out the clouds and come on Stink."

I turned my attention towards him and realized we were in front of my building. I rolled my eyes at him and got out the car.

"Wait, hol' up; you not gonna say bye or nothing?" Kashmir asked, getting out the car and sitting on the hood.

"I thought you was coming upstairs, are you not?"

"Nah, I got some business I need to handle."

"How am I supposed to get to your mom's shop?" I questioned, walking back towards him.

"Why you got all this space in between us? Come here Azuri." I walked over to him slowly but it wasn't fast enough because he snatched me up real quick.

"When I tell you to get here, you get here, not take yo fucking time. Why you keep playing with me like I won't fuck yo little ass up?"

"Maybe I want you to fuck me up daddy," I purred.

"I knew you was into that domestic violence shit. You gonna have me out here acting like Chris Brown."

"Boy please, you aren't half as fine as Chris Brown." I smiled.

"You must wanna see R.I.P to that nigga all over social media."

"Stop it."

"Fuck all that shit, take my car to my mom's shop and I'll have Jahzir come get me."

"You sure?" I questioned. I have drove Kashmir's car before but it was always with him riding shot gun.

"You good to drive, right? I don't need you fucking up my shit."

"Your little car will be fine but let me go before I'm late for my first day."

"Iight, make sure you're at my crib later. Scoop your moms and we can have a movie night or something."

"Okay, you got it."

Kashy gave me a kiss and, I swear, I didn't want it to end. When his tongue slipped into my mouth, I was ready to take this whole thing up to the crib.

"Come upstairs with me for a quickie," I moaned against his mouth.

"I thought you didn't want to be late," he smirked.

"I'll be late if it means I can feel you deep inside of me."

A response wasn't needed after that and Kashmir never gave one. He wrapped his arms around my waist, leading me over to my building. We made out during the elevator ride like a couple of teenagers. When we got to my apartment, I unlocked the door, ready to have Kashmir explore my body.

"Hold up Azuri!" Kashmir said, pulling me behind him.

"What happened?" I asked

"Where that small box come from that's on your counter?"

I looked at the counter and there was indeed a small black box. "I don't know. I don't think it was there when we left."

"Stay right here?" He went over to the black box and me being the person I am, I followed him.

"Yo ass don't fucking listen." He sighed.

"Just open the box," I told him, rolling my eyes.

He opened the box, only to find a single bullet with his name in engraved. "What is that?" I asked him. It was a stupid question but I needed answers.

"None of your business; don't worry about it," he spat. I watched him pull out his gun, then search my entire apartment. The search didn't take long because my house wasn't that big to begin with.

"Go pack you and your mother some shit. Y'all staying with me," he demanded.

"Before I pack anything, I need you to explain to me what is going on."

"Now isn't the fucking time to question me, Azuri. Go pack yo shit like I fucking told you to!"

"Fuck you, Kashmir," I told him and stomped towards my mother's room.

There was no need for Kashmir to be mad. All I was trying to do was figure out what the fuck was going, since someone had obviously got into my apartment. I packed all of the things my mother would need then went to go pack mine. I finished and Kashmir took both bags, leading the way out the door. I locked up then quickly sent my mom a text, telling her to be ready by the time I pulled up. I wasn't sure what was going on but I damn sure wasn't going to leave my mother at my aunt's house in the blind.

Chapter 22: Gotti

This muthafucka had balls of steel! Not only did he break into my girl's crib, but he sent me a silent threat that I didn't take lightly. I didn't know who this muthafucka was, but he had started a got damn war that I don't think he was ready for. I completely tuned Azuri out; her little ass was mad, but I didn't give a fuck at the moment.

"Kashmir, you need to tell me what's goin on!" she shouted.

"Yo, on the real ma, I need you to cool that shit right now. I ain't got no time to explain," I replied calmly while dialing Jahzir.

"Yo!" he answered.

"You know where Naomi hood at, right?" I asked.

"Yea, what's up, what happened?"

"Meet me there in fifteen," I replied, hanging up before he could respond.

I gripped the steering wheel so tight that my knuckles turned white. I was on a thousand and murder was the only thing on my mind. Azuri was talking, but I had tunnel vision, so that shit was going in one ear and out the other.

Finally pulling up to Naomi's building, I was glad as hell to see Jah waiting for me. I turned to a pissed off Azuri and grabbed her face gently, turning her toward me. Everything that I was about to say, she needed to hear and pay close attention to.

"What you gon do right now is go get your mother, then you gonna go to my crib and wait for me. I'll call my dukes and let her know something came up, so you ain't gon be able to make it. Megan is gon meet you there in a little bit; she has a key and she knows the code. If, for any reason, somebody gets past the gate and knocks on the door, don't answer that shit. In my room, by that window that you like to sit at so much is an imaginary button. Your fingerprints are already programmed in it, so just feel for the button, push it, and the floor will open up. Go down into the panic room and wait until I come get you. It's equipped with everything you need, including security monitors, so you'll be able to see what's going on. Understand?"

"Kashy, what's goin on, you're scaring me," she said, panicking.

"I need you to calm down and relax Stink, can you do that for me?"

She nodded her head and steadied her breathing.

"That's my girl." I winked.

"Baby, please tell me what's going on," she cried.

"It's about to be mayhem," I told her and with that, I climbed out of the car.

Nala was coming out the door with a confused look on her face as she approached me.

"What the hell y'all doing back here? I know that damn daughter of mine didn't-"

"Nala, I need you to listen to everything I'm bout to tell you," I started before I ran down everything that happened.

Her skin turned red and her eyes got dark.

"I need you to go to my house with Azuri; she knows what to do in case of an emergency. There are guns stashed all over my house. I see your gangsta, so I know you know what to do," I smirked before running down all the stash spots at my house.

"I got it son, you be careful out there and make sure you bring your black ass back because if anything happens to you, it will kill my baby," she told me sternly.

"I'm good Nala," I replied.

"Ok, I'm gon trust your word baby," she said, hugging me.

Making my way to the car, I opened the passenger door and pulled Azuri out.

"You remember what I told you, right?" I asked her, wrapping my arms around her waist.

She nodded her head with tears in her eyes. Wiping them away before they could fall, I gently kissed her lips.

"Chill Stink, everything gon be good ma," I reassured her.

"You don't know that though Kashy, what if something goes wrong?" she asked, looking into my eyes.

"Then just make sure you bury me a G," I joked.

"That's not funny Kashmir." She glared at me.

"Nah, but on some real shit, you remember what I told you last night?"

She nodded her head.

"What I say?" I quizzed.

"You said that knowing I'm waiting on you is motivation for you to make it home every night," she quoted.

"That's right and that ain't changed Stink, you my lifeline ma." I kissed her.

"Promise me you'll be careful," she replied.

"Always." I nodded.

"I love you, Kashmir," she told me.

"I love you more, Stink." I winked before kissing her lips softly.

Pulling away, I ushered her and her mother into the truck before making my way to Jah's whip. I watched them safely pull away, then hopped in the car with my brother.

"What's the word big bruh?" he asked.

I ran down what happened at Azuri's crib to my brother and he damn near spazzed.

"Yo, this muthafucka gotta die bruh, he got balls though; I give him that," Jah spat.

"Ain't nobody got no info on his ass?" I asked, lighting a blunt.

"Nah, not yet, but we can always go to pops, man." He shrugged.

"Hell no, he left us in charge and I ain't goin to his ass unless I absolutely have to. We can solve this shit on our own Jah; the streets gon talk soon enough," I told him.

I was a nigga with pride and, most importantly, I was a grown ass man. My pops handed this shit over to us for a reason, so I knew that we could handle this shit. The easy thing to do would've been going to my pops, but fuck it. I was a nigga that liked to do shit the hard way; it was more fun.

"I feel you, bruh." Jah nodded. "Quest rounded up the crew and put the word out that there was fifty racks to the first mu'fucka that brought us info on this Tamir nigga," he added.

I nodded my head and pulled on the blunt before passing it to Jah. For the next few hours, we combed the streets looking for info on this nigga, but nobody knew shit. This nigga was like a fuckin ghost or some shit.

"Aye, didn't pops say that nigga was from Philly or some shit?" I asked.

"Yea, I think so, why what's up?"

"Maybe nobody knows his ass because his life is in Philly," I replied.

Jah looked at me and smirked; it was then that I knew he was thinking what I was thinking.

"Down for a road trip?" we asked in unison before laughing like hell.

"You know I'm wit it big bruh, just let me know when." He shrugged.

"Aight, then we leave in a day or two. Quest, Dru, and Smoke gon roll wit us. We gon hit his town incognito, see how shit moving down there, and see what info we come up with. Then we gon wipe his muthafuckin traps out," I spat heatedly.

I didn't need his drugs or his money, but I knew that would bring his slick ass out of hiding. He thought he was smart, but there was more than one way to skin a cat and I was gonna do it the old fashioned way. I was gon hit that nigga pockets.

"Aye, you know that nigga Deon live up in Philly now," Jah told me.

"Oh yea?" I asked, stroking my chin hair in deep thought.

"Hit that nigga line and tell him we gon be in his city soon; maybe his ass can give us some insight on this nigga," I added.

"Fa'sho, I'll hit em up tomorrow," he replied.

"Let's roll man, I need to go lay up under my girl," I told him.

"Listen at yo ass gettin soft and shit." Jah laughed.

"Shit, I can't believe myself." I laughed, shaking my head.

"Love will do that to a gangsta quick," he replied and I nodded my head in agreement.

"She a good look for you bruh, she genuine and moms like her, so you know that's a plus. Remember when she met Dionna's ass?"

"Man, how could I forget." I shook my head.

Dionna was a chick that I was dealing with heavy about five years ago. At the time, I wasn't looking to settle down, but Dionna was something like my main chick. After dealing with each other for almost a year, she wanted to meet my dukes, so I agreed. It would come to be the biggest mistake I ever made.

My dukes hurt her feelings so got damn bad and cursed me out in the process. Shit wild though, cause everything my dukes said about her ass was the truth.

"Get yo ugly ass out bitch," Jah said, snapping me out of my thoughts.

"I got yo bitch, nigga," I replied, getting out the car and squaring up.

We threw a few jabs at each other while laughing, both of us high as all hell. Finally making our way into the house, I fell out laughing at the sight of Nala patrolling through with a gun in her hand and one in the small of her back.

"Nala, you think you GI Jane or some shit?" I asked.

"Nigga, you better ask about me. I ain't new to this, I'm true to this. But since you're back, here you go," she said, handing me the guns. "I saw you got one of them whirlpool tubs upstairs and I can't wait to try it out, so deuces," she added, climbing the stairs without another word.

"What did you do to my mother?"

"I ain't do nothin, yo mama a G, Stink," I smirked at Azuri, pulling her up onto my lap and burying my face in her neck.

"You wanna tell me what's going on now?"

"Yea and I need to know too. You got me fucked up Jahzir, cause the way you snapped at me on the phone earlier almost got you cussed under," Megan spat.

"Man, sit yo lil ass down some got damn where," Jah said, sucking his teeth.

"Who the fuck you talkin to, Jah? Cause it can't be me, make me embarrass yo ass in front of yo brother; play like you don't know what it is." She glared, daring him to say something.

His ass got quiet real quick.

"Got damn bruh, let me find out Megan run that shit," I smirked.

He sucked his teeth and flipped me the bird, but didn't say shit. Megan had that nigga on lock, she got away with a lot of shit. I wish the fuck Azuri would try that shit with me.

I ran down everything to both of them, from the time my pops told us about this nigga, up until he left the bullet at Azuri's house. I could tell Azuri was pissed because her whole body trembled.

"So, with that being said, you and your mother ain't goin back to that house. It was too easy for him to get into your crib; your mother already got shot behind this shit and I'll be damned if anything happens to one of y'all again," I told her.

She didn't reply, which was surprising, she simply nodded her head in agreement. We talked and chilled for a minute, but I could tell my Stink was in her feelings. Once my brother and Megan left, I led her upstairs and to my room. She had to check on her mother first, but once she saw her sleeping peacefully, she walked in my room and closed the door.

I sat her down on the bed and made my way into the bathroom to run a bubble bath in the Jacuzzi styled tub. I didn't really do all the bubbles and shit, but I would do anything for my Stink. Once the tub was filled, I walked back into the room and stripped her out of her clothes, both of us in silence.

Leading her to the bathroom, I helped her into the tub and dimmed the lights, lighting the candles around the tub. I stripped and slid in behind her.

"What's on your mind Stink?" I asked her, after we sat in silence for a while.

"I don't want to lose you, Kashmir, I just got you and I'm not ready to let you go yet," she said softly.

"I ain't goin nowhere ma, at least I'm tryin not to, but if something does happen to me, you gon be good."

"Don't talk like that Kashy," she replied.

"I'm just keepin it a band, ma. Every time I walk out that door, it ain't no guarantee that I'll make it back, but I'm damn sure gon try. Look Stink, you know what I do and you know my lifestyle is dangerous. I ain't scared to die ma, but I ain't goin nowhere no time soon. I love you too much to let you go," I told her honestly.

"I know and I love you too, this shit is just crazy, like something out of a movie or some shit." She sighed.

"It comes with the territory; right now it's either kill or be killed and I ain't tryin to be on the receiving end. Fuck all that shit though, you tryin to pop this pussy for a real nigga?" I whispered in her ear, licking her earlobe and making her shiver.

"You so damn nasty," she moaned, as my fingers found her center.

"Yea, but you like that shit though," I told her before lifting her slightly and sliding her down on me.

"Sssssss…" she hissed and I bit my lip to keep from crying out like a bitch.

She rocked her hips slowly, throwing her head back against my chest. I bit down on her neck gently and tweaked her nipples with my fingers.

"Shit Stink," I groaned, as she locked her muscles down on me.

Leaning forward slightly, she grabbed onto my legs and bounced lightly, causing the water to swoosh like waves. Sliding my finger in her ass, I could tell I caught her off guard because she jumped a little, but didn't slow down her movements.

"I'm gonna cum baby!" she cried out.

"Let that shit go then ma," I groaned.

Her body shook and her pussy gripped my dick tighter, causing my eyes to roll up into my head. I wasn't ready to cum, but the way she was twerking on my dick made that shit damn near impossible. She slid up to the tip and rode that shit before slamming her ass back down on me; that sent me over the edge.

I grabbed her hips and fucked her from the bottom, not giving a damn about the water getting on the floor. Moments later, I released my seed so deep inside her that I knew she was pregnant with my junior.

"Got damn I love yo ass Stink, but I think I love that pussy more," I panted, still buried inside her.

She panted and giggled, trying to catch her breath. My dick bricked back up and I grinded into her from the bottom. I slapped her ass for her to get up, then helped her out the tub and bent her over the side. Sliding balls deep inside her pussy, I commenced to tearing that ass all the way up.

I was on a mission to get her lil ass pregnant tonight, fuck what you heard!

Chapter 23: Azuri

"Azuri, I'm about to leave out; you sure you will be okay closing up by yourself?" Gina asked me.

"Yeah, I'll be fine. I'll call you to let you know when I'm leaving so you know everything went fine."

"No need baby, I know you got this. You have been working your ass off, picking up everything."

"I just want to make sure that I know all there is to know. I don't want to let anyone down."

"You couldn't let me down even if you tried. You are a bright young lady."

"Thank you." I smiled.

"You are very welcome. I'm going to swing by the house to pick up your mother. We are supposed to go to the casino out and queens tonight."

"Sound like fun, enjoy yourselves and make sure you tell my mom to behave."

"Why would I do a thing like that when I don't plan on behaving myself." Gina laughed, walking out the door.

All I could do was shake my head at Gina. In the past week that my mother and I have been staying with Kashmir, my mother and Gina became as thick as thieves. Whenever Gina wasn't at work, she was with my mother and vice versa. There were even times where my mother came up to the job just to help Gina out. I was glad the two of them were getting along but at the same time, I wanted my mother to sit still. Speaking of sitting still, I have barley seen Kashmir in the past week. He was always gone by the time I woke up and always came in when I was sleeping. I didn't nag or question his whereabouts; I would just send him text messages throughout the day, letting him know I was thinking of him. A lot of the time my texts would go unanswered and it bothered me, but I never brought it up. Everything that was happening came with the territory of being with a man of Kashmir's status; I just hoped that he realized sooner than later that I was starting to feel neglected.

Trying not to think of Kashmir, I busied myself around the store helping customers and things of that nature. The shoe store his mom owned was big but it wasn't too big, so there was only really two people in the store at a time working. Me and the sales associate Brydell made sure that all the customers left with a smile on their face.

"Brydell, hold down the floor, I'm about to go in the back for a second."

"Okay, no problem."

I went into the back office and sat down for a second. I was trying not to think of Kashmir but he kept popping up in my head. I pulled out my phone and dialed his number, but it went straight to voicemail. I tried calling one more time but ended up with the same result as before. Now, this wasn't the first time my calls had went to voicemail when I called Kashmir, but something wasn't sitting right with me. I tried calling one last time; instead of the phone ringing out and going to voicemail, it just went straight to voicemail.

"This asshole," I said out loud.

I was about to go back into the front when something told me to call Megan.

"Hey chicka, wassup. I thought you were at work," she said, sounding cheerful as hell.

"I am at work. Is Jahzir with you?" If Jahzir was with Megan, that mean Kashmir was up to something.

"No, him and Gotti left for Philly this morning. Gotti didn't tell you?"

"No, his ass didn't tell me. I barley even see him anymore." I sighed into the phone.

"Don't stress it Zuri. Gotti isn't used to having a girl by his side while he is trying to make moves."

"I know you're only trying to comfort me but what you just said is some bullshit. I understand him being out in the streets trying to get whoever the dude is that's trying to get at him; what I don't understand is how he can forget about me all in the process. The nigga doesn't reach out to me or nothing during the day. I'm the one that always have to send a text or call, just to hear that nigga's voice. You can't tell me that if Jahzir was doing the same thing, you would be okay with it?"

"You're right, I wouldn't be okay with it. At the same time, you have to tell him how you feel. You think you're doing the right thing by not saying anything or nagging but, in reality, you're hurting yourself. Gotti isn't a mind reader Azuri."

"I know he isn't but I also shouldn't have to teach him how to be attentive. Like, all I'm asking is for a quick I love you text during the day." I slightly laughed.

"When bullets be flying, no nigga got time to be sending texts girl."

"Wait, someone shot at him?" At that point, all the anger I felt towards Kashmir was replaced by concern.

"No, it was just an example girl. Gotti loves you and even though he hasn't been around, his love for you hasn't faded. Let's go out tonight because it's apparent you need some fun in yo life."

"I was supposed to go over to my aunt's house and chill with Naomi. She complaining about how we don't spend time together."

"I though y'all wasn't close?"

"We're not." I laughed. Naomi was full of shit; the only reason why I agreed to chill with her was because Kashmir wasn't going to be home and my mom was always with Gina, which left me alone every night after work.

"Tell her ass we're going to the club; you know she wouldn't miss a chance to be seen."

"You are right about that one. Let me call her and see what she says."

"Ok, just come straight to my house after work so we can get dressed, then we can just go scoop her."

"Okay, sounds good to me."

We said our good byes then hung up the phone. I was about to call Naomi when Brydell came knocking on the door.

"There is a customer out here asking for you by name."

"Okay, I'm coming now." I got up, locked the office, then went towards the front.

I wanted to believe that Kashmir was out there trying to surprise me, but I quickly found out that wasn't the truth when I saw Naomi standing there.

"Heyy cousin, I was in the area and wanted to make sure that we were still on for tonight."

"I was just about to call you about that-" I started, but she didn't waste any time cutting me off.

"Don't tell me you're skipping out on me because of Gotti's ass," she sassed, rolling her neck.

"Gotti is out of town, so he's not that the reason and I'm not skipping out on you. If your rude ass would've let me finish, I would've been able to tell you that we were going to the club tonight with Megan."

"Eh, I don't know," she said, rolling her eyes.

"What are you being extra for?"

"I'm not a fan of Megan."

"Why not?"

"Just something about her rubs me the wrong way but I guess if you want to go to the club, we can do that." She shrugged.

"That's exactly what I want to do, so I guess that's what we are going to do." I was already upset about Kashmir going to Philly without telling me and I didn't need nor want to deal with Naomi's mini attitude.

"No need to get slick, Azuri. I said if that's what you want to do then that's what we are going to do."

"I'm getting dressed at Megan's house. We can pick you up or you can just meet us."

"You can just pick me up because I don't feel like driving."

"Okay," I told her, then got back to work.

Naomi stayed for a little while longer then she left. I didn't know what her problem with Megan was but I was going to find out. I made a mental note to ask Megan if her and my cousin had any run ins. The rest of my work day went pretty quickly. After cleaning up the store and counting the money, I looked over the sales receipts to make sure that we at least hit our goal. To my surprise, we went over our goal by five grand. I was happy as hell; I tried calling Kashmir again but still got no answer. I decided to just stop trying because every time I tried, nothing was happening but me getting my feelings hurt. Tonight, I was going to go out and celebrate while putting all thoughts of Kashmir on the back burner. Tonight was solely about me.

* * * *

"He got a good thing goin with a bad bitch. He knows who to call when he need it. Wish I had another you, I'm greedy. Sometimes like that nigga get greedy. Got damn he fell in love with a bad bitch. He knows that every time he leaves me. Even though I know how men be talkin. I just know that bitch wanna be me. He came up in here and fell in love with a bad bitch."

I was in the club rapping along to French Montana's song Bad Bitch, having the time of my life. Megan, Naomi, and I were on the dance floor going in. We had drinks in our hands and our asses were clapping. A couple of times dudes tried to dance with me, but I politely declined because I wasn't here for that. I may have been mad at Kashmir but I was still going to represent him regardless.

"Is that Gotti?" Naomi asked out of nowhere, killing my buzz.

"Stop trying to be messy; Gotti is in Philly," Megan said.

"No, he is not; he is right across the room with a bitch on his lap," Naomi said, twirling her neck.

I looked in the direction Naomi was pointing in and, lo and behold, Kashmir was over there with some foreign looking bitch on his lap.

Chapter 24: Gotti

Takin the trip to Philly was a good move. I got a little info on this Tamir cat and hit three of his traps in a matter of eight hours. I knew that once Tamir found out I was responsible for his spots being stashed, he was gon retaliate, but I would be waiting for his bitch ass. Hell, I told his lil workers to let him know that it was Gotti that took his shit; well, the ones that I didn't kill anyway. I didn't need his shit, but I knew that would be a way to bring his ass out

I had my phone turned off the whole time I was gone, so I knew Azuri was gon spazz on my ass the minute I hit the door. The only reason I didn't tell her about the Philly trip is because I didn't want her to worry; plus, I knew I wouldn't be gone that long.

We got back to the city around ten and I somehow let these niggas talk me into going out, instead of takin my black ass home like I started too. I was in the middle of a conversation with Dru when this chick I used to fuck with name Chantel came and sat on my lap.

"The fuck is you doin ma?" I asked, looking at her ass like she had lost her fuckin mind.

"Damn Gotti, it's like that?" she asked, turning her face up.

Chantel was a bad ass mixed bitch, but she was needy as fuck and wanted more than I was willing to offer her ass.

"It's just like that, so I need you to remove yourself; I got a lady now ma," I said before gently nudging her to get her ass the fuck up off me.

A nigga may have done a lot of things, but cheating on Azuri was some shit I just wasn't gon do. It wasn't a bitch in the world that could make me fuck up what I had at the crib.

"Ah shit!" Jah spat, looking past me.

Just as Chantel was getting up, I turned my head and came face to face with Azuri.

"Ah fuck," I mumbled under my breath.

"So, this is what the fuck we on Kashmir?" she asked with her hands on her wide hips.

"It ain't what it look like ma, I swear to God it ain't," I told her, standing up.

"Oh no? Cause it looked to me as if you had a bitch on ya lap, like you ain't got a girl at home. Then, on top of that, I been calling you all fuckin day and not once did you answer! What takes the cake for me though is that you were supposed to be in Philly. So, please explain to me what the fuck it is, cause I know what the fuck my eyes saw," she spat angrily.

"Fuck all that, the fuck is yo simple ass doin out the house anyway? Didn't I tell you not to go nowhere?" I gritted.

"Don't try to flip this shit around on me Kashmir, answer my got damn question!"

Rubbing my hand down my face, I looked at Jah for help and this punk ass nigga just shrugged. To make matters worse, Chantel was still standing beside me.

"Ayo, get the fuck on! Yo ass done caused enough trouble for tonight!" I spat at her ass.

"Fuck you Gotti, don't be mad at me cause yo bitch caught you slippin!"

"Nah, fuck you ma, ain't nobody even tell you to sit yo ass on my fuckin lap in the first place. Now, you tryin to make it seem like it was somethin that it wasn't, move the fuck around Tel!"

A nigga was heated and this bitch was bout two point five seconds from being choked the fuck out. She sucked her teeth and rolled her eyes before stomping out of VIP.

"I know you tight wit a nigga Stink, but believe me when I say it wasn't nothing goin on ma," I told Azuri, getting in her space.

"So, I'm supposed to believe that?" she asked, folding her arms across her chest.

"Yea." I shrugged.

"Nigga, you got me fucked up! I don't know what kind of weak ass bitches you used to dealing with, but Azuri ain't the one you can game. I know what the fuck I saw and even though you *claim* she just sat down on yo lap, you should've pushed her off, but you entertained that bitch. What if I wouldn't have caught you huh, then what?"

"Then nothing, cause wasn't shit happenin! You can ask any muthafucka in here what happened and they'll tell you the same thing I'm tellin you. The fuck I look like cheatin wit a off brand bitch, when I got the full package at home? A nigga my play crazy, but I ain't that got damn crazy," I told her seriously.

She tried to hide the small smile that tugged at the corners of her mouth, but she couldn't. Rolling her eyes, she sucked her teeth and stared at me long and hard.

"Don't fuckin play with me Kashmir Banks, cause I ain't that bitch. The next time a bitch even try to come within two feet of yo ass, you better push that bitch back. I'm gon take yo word for what happened; just don't let that shit happen again. I would hate to have to nut up on yo fuckin ass. Plus, I'm still mad about you not answering my calls and telling me you was goin out of town."

"My bad ma, I had to handle business and I turned my phone off. I was in the wrong and I apologize, you forgive me?" I asked, wrapping my arms around her waist and pulling her into me.

"I don't know yet," she smirked.

"Yea aight, fuck wit it Stink," I smirked back before kissing her full lips.

"You ready to dip?" I asked, ready to go home and slide up in her sexy ass.

"Yea, I'm ready," she told me.

I went to let my niggas know I was leaving and walked up on a full blown argument. Megan was letting Jah have it, but he wasn't backing down; the shit was downright comical.

"Keep fuckin playin wit me Jah and I'm gon nut the fuck up on yo stupid ass! You know how I get down, so I don't even know why you keep tryin it wit me!" Megan spat.

"Man, you better sit you light bright lookin ass the fuck down some got damn where before I put my foot in yo ass!"

"I wish the fuck you would! Nigga, I will cut your got damn ass from asshole to appetite!"

I couldn't do shit but laugh, cause that shit made absolutely no fuckin sense.

"I'm out," I said, dapping my niggas up.

"Me too, for I have to fuck Megan lil ass up in here," Jah said, standing up.

Grabbing Azuri, I pulled her lil ass through the club with Naomi, Jah, and Megan behind us.

"Umm, how am I supposed to get home?" Naomi asked, once we made it outside.

"Yo fuckin feet don't look broke to me." Jah laughed.

"What the fuck ever Jahzir; I rode here with Megan and somebody gon take me home."

"Call fuckin Uber mu'fucka," I spat, ready to get away from her ass.

Naomi rubbed me the wrong way and even though I knew she was Azuri's cousin, I didn't trust that bitch not one bit.

"Stop bein mean Kashy," Azuri said, punching me in my arm.

"Aye, yo lil ass better chill wit all that hittin and shit," I warned.

She waved me off before telling Naomi we would take her home.

"You must be hard of hearing or some shit Stink; I'm not lettin that sneaky bitch ride in shit of mine. Her ass better call a Uber or some shit," I spat angrily.

"Seriously Kashmir?"

"As a fuckin heart attack," I replied before heading to my truck and climbing inside.

I watched her in the rearview mirror as she talked to Naomi and then hugged her before making her way to the truck.

"You don't have to be so mean to her," she told me.

"Look Stink, I know that's yo fam and all, but quite frankly, I don't like that hoe or trust her. She got some shit wit her, ma; you better watch her ass!" I said, pulling away from the curb.

"Whatever," she said, waving me off. "So, you wanna tell me why you had to go to Philly?" she asked, changing the subject.

"I told you, business," I told her.

"What kind of business?"

"The fuck is you the FEDs or some shit?" I asked, eyeing her.

"Shut the fuck up Kashmir! I wanna know what the fuck is goin on; I'm apparently involved in this shit, so I need to know," she argued.

I sighed heavily and grabbed a pre-rolled blunt out the console. Sparking it up, I debated on whether or not I wanted to fill her in on all the shit that's going on. On one hand, I didn't want her involved in this shit, but on the other hand, I didn't want her walking around blind either. Passing her the blunt, I said fuck it and ran down the whole situation to her.

She listened intently without saying a word, as we passed the blunt back and forth. When I was done, she didn't say anything for a while. Just as we were pulling into the driveway, she started talking.

"I trust you enough to know that you'll protect us at all cost, but I think it's time that I learned how to use a gun. Before you protest, just hear me out first. I don't want to be walking around blindly and possibly be in a fucked up situation without any protection. It would be stupid of me to think that you would be glued to my side twenty-four hours a day. In this lifestyle, I know that they'll use the ones closest to you in order to hurt you; I don't want to be in that situation. Teach me how to be yo Bonnie baby, cause I promise you ain't another muthafucka out here gon have yo back like me. I'm ya rider baby, so teach me," she said.

I ain't gon lie, at first I was apprehensive, but the more she talked, the more she made sense and made my dick hard in the process. Even though I didn't want her holding court in the streets with me or nothing like that, I wanted her to be able to protect herself whenever I wasn't around.

"Aight Stink, I'm gon teach your lil ass, but only for yo protection. I don't want you runnin round here tryin to be like those gansta bitches you read about," I said, causing her to laugh.

"I'm serious Stink," I told her.

"I know Kashy and I understand baby, just teach me," she said softly before kissing my lips.

Deepening the kiss, I slid my seat back and pulled her onto my lap. Biting down on her neck, she moaned as her hands unfastened my belt buckle. Taking my dick out, she slid her panties to the side and slid down on my shit so fast, I damn near screamed out like a bitch.

The only sounds that could be heard were moans and skin slapping, as we fucked each other with a vengeance. I was on the verge of cumming when I saw headlights pulling through the gate. Azuri was in her own little world and the way her eyes were rolling, her little ass wasn't seeing shit.

"Oooohhh, I'm cummin baby!" she cried out, squeezing the life out of my dick.

The nut came rushing out of me and deep into her, as the car pulled up beside me. I noticed that it was my duke's car and tapped Azuri to get up, just as Nala stepped out the car.

"Mmm hmm, y'all nasty asses couldn't even wait til you got in the house, I saw that got damn truck rockin from the gate." She laughed.

"Oh my God," Azuri said, covering her face as I laughed and cracked the window some.

"Bring y'all nasty asses on in this house!" she said before telling my mother bye and walking in the house.

My dukes shook her head laughing, while pulling around the circle and disappearing back out the gate.

"Come on ma," I told Azuri, stuffing my dick back in my pants.

"I can't face my mama after this Kashy," she whined.

"Girl get yo big grown ass out the car, it ain't like she don't know you fuckin." I laughed.

Punching me in the arm, Azuri climbed out and did the walk of shame all the way to the door.

"All I know is, if you get pregnant, you better hire a nanny cause mama done got her groove back!" Nala said from the top of the stairs.

I laughed and shook my head; her ass was off the chain. Azuri tip toed up the stairs like her ass was gon get a whooping or some shit. We showered and hit the bed; I pulled Azuri onto my chest and a nigga was out in seconds.

Chapter 25: Azuri

The sun was shining, the birds were chirping, and Kashmir was still in bed when I woke up this morning. I slowly slipped out of bed, trying my best not to wake him. He stirred but not once opened his eyes. Handling my morning breath and the crust that was in my eyes was the first thing on my to-do list for the day. Thirty minutes later, I emerged from the bathroom with a towel wrapped around my body.

I quickly lotioned my body, then threw on a pair of Kashmir's boxers along with my Pink sports bra. I grabbed my kindle and phone before walking out the room, leaving Kashmir to sleep.

"Uh ma, where the hell do you think you're going?" I guess it was a good thing I made the decision to make breakfast because I caught my mom trying to sneak out the kitchen side door.

"Azuri, what are you doing up so early?"

"It's not early, it's ten, ma; where were you trying to go?" I asked again.

"I just wanted to get out and get some fresh air."

"Nala, where are you, girl? You was supposed to been ready and what did you pack in all of these bags?" I heard Gina complain from the other side of the door.

I walked around the bar area, so I could get a better view as to what was going on. "Oh hey Azuri, I closed down the store for the weekend because me and your mother is going away and I figured you and Kashy could use some time alone." Gina smiled

"Ma, when was you going to tell me that your ass is going on vacation?" I crossed my arms over my chest, trying not to overdo it. Since Gina and my mom hooked up, I wasn't as on her as I was before. I was giving her more room to do as she pleased but I felt now she was taking advantage.

"I was going to send you a text." She smiled, as if that was the million-dollar answer.

"How would you feel if I just up and left and I only sent you a text?"

"I would be okay because you're grown, as am I. I know you worry about me sweetie but what's for me is for me and if it's death, then I have no choice but to welcome it. Baby, we both have to live our life like it's our last. I love you, Azuri."

"I love you too, ma." I sighed. I gave her a hug and a kiss, then watched her carry her last bag to the car.

"Azuri, stop worrying; your mother may have an illness but that doesn't mean she has to behave as such. You can't keep her locked up in the house. She knows her limits and, trust me, she has never gone over them when I'm around. Let your mother live because you don't want her to die with regrets."

Gina gave me a hug then went and jumped in the car with my mom. A couple of tears fell from my eyes unexpectedly. I wiped them away quickly because Gina was right; I needed to let my mother live, so she wouldn't die with regrets. Since it was just Kashmir and I for the day, I decided to cook him breakfast and bring it to him in bed.

I figured it was the least I could do for how I been acting with him lately. He might not have said it but I knew this hard exterior I had was fucking with him a little. It was like we were both struggling to be on top in this relationship, not to mention I was always over reacting and doing the most when it came to certain situations. I needed to let go and believe and trust that Kashy had my best interest at heart.

It didn't take long for me to prepare the pancakes, cheese eggs, grits, and bacon. I made both of us a plate, along with some juice. I was about to bring the tray of food upstairs when I thought about him may wanting a blunt. I swiped his car keys off the counter and ran out the door. I looked in the glove compartment and there were about three rolled blunts. I took one out and shook my head. This nigga was something else.

I ran back in the house, grabbed his food along with the lighter, and headed up the stairs. I expected Kashmir to still be sleep but he was up talking on the phone.

"Nah, if you need anything hit up Jahzir. Don't question what the fuck I just said nigga. Yo, on the real, you can either do as I say or your oxygen will be cut off in 2.5. The choice is yours. Yeah, I thought you would see it my way, get the fuck off my phone." He was eyeing me and licking his lips, like he was about to devour me and this food.

"Damn Stink, that's all for me?"

"Yeah." I passed him the tray of food and sat at the edge of the bed studying him. It was hard to explain Kashy but, at the same time, so easy. He was so complex, yet, so simple.

"Stink, I know you didn't roll this; where you get it from?" he questioned, examining the blunt.

"From your car Kashmir." I rolled my eyes because I was feeling like he was trying to play me.

"Chill with the attitude before I fuck you up," he warned.

"Kashy, you're too soft to fuck me up, so cut the tough boy act."

"Ain't shit soft about me, not even my dick," he smirked, pulling the cover back to show me his hard on.

"You're so annoying." I stole a piece of bacon of his plate and went to put it in my mouth when he snatched it from me.

"Damn, it was just one piece of bacon."

"It was my bacon." He laughed.

I sat there fake pouting, waiting to see if he would give me the piece of bacon back. This asshole never even looked back in my direction. I got off the bed and stomped my way into the kitchen. I sat at the table, eating the plate of food I made for myself before I brought Kashy his. I scrolled on Facebook while I ate, just to give myself something to do. I stumbled upon one of Naomi's post. It rubbed me the wrong way because it was about family and I was the only family she really had. I scrolled my contact list looking for her number.

"I knew it would only be a matter of time before you called," Naomi answered the phone sounding salty as hell.

"Do you need some fries for all that salt you got over there?"

"Haha, very funny Azuri but you called me, so what do you want?"

"I called you to find out about that funny post you made. Why can't you trust family Naomi?"

"I had to spend money I didn't have just to get home last night."

"I'm sorry about that Naomi; you act like you have never left me hanging before."

"I may have left you hanging before but I never allowed dudes to disrespect you."

"That's because I don't give them a reason to disrespect me. I carry myself in a way that makes dudes respect me. You, on the other hand, are always walking around with your ass and titties hanging out. How do you expect anyone to respect you when you don't respect yourself Naomi?"

"If I wanted a lecture, I would've talked to my mother," Naomi spat.

"Who you talking to?" Kashmir asked, coming into the kitchen. Before I could answer his question, he snatched my phone away from me.

"Who this?"

"Gotti, I was trying to have a conversation with my cousin, not you. Put her back on the phone."

"Naomi, you know how a nigga gets down. Watch your fucking tone when you talking to me. Matter of fact, lose this number." He hung up the phone then turned towards me. "I don't want you chilling with her anymore."

"Kashmir, you can't tell me who I can and can't chill with," I snapped.

"Yes I can and I just did."

"Kashmir, that's not fair," I whined. I wasn't close with Naomi and, yeah, she got on my nerves, but she was still my family.

"I don't give a fuck about shit being fair. You don't want no bitches in my face and I don't want you around your cousin. As far as I see it, that shit is fair as fuck."

"That is two different things."

"Azuri, stop trying to fight me on this. I don't want you fucking with her; she shady as fuck and I don't need you mixed in anything that has to be do with her."

"Fine," I said, giving in.

I got up, cleaning up the mess that I made while I was cooking. I started doing the dishes when Gotti wrapped his arms around my waist.

"Don't be upset Stink, I'm just doing this for your benefit. You may not see it now but in the long run, you will."

"I'm not worried about nothing, I trust you."

"Say that shit again, Stink."

"I trust you." I giggled. "Let me finish cleaning up so I can start my day."

"The fuck you mean start your day; I know you heard me on the phone. I'm spending the day getting you pregnant."

"Oh, you were serious. I thought that was a joke." I laughed.

"I'm not the joking type and you should already know that. Bring yo ass upstairs when you're finished, so I can slide up in it." He smacked my ass then walked away.

I didn't care how serious Kashmir was about us having babies, I didn't think I was ready for that. We were gonna talk about the situation when the time was right because I needed us to be on the same page. But, for now, I was going to enjoy all of my baby's loving.

Chapter 26: Naomi

"Oooh yes baby, right there!" I moaned, throwing my ass back.

He smacked my ass and went even deeper, causing me to roll my eyes up in my head. Slipping his finger into my ass sent me over the top. This nigga was breaking me off something serious and I was loving every minute of it.

"Got damn yo pussy good as fuck ma," he groaned.

We had been going at it for damn near two hours and I had lost track of how many times I came.

"Ah fuck! Come catch this shit ma!" he growled before pulling out.

Quickly turning around and dropping to my knees, I took his dick in my mouth and sucked the nut off, swallowing every drop.

"Shit Nay, you gon fuck around and make a nigga wife yo ass up!" he said, panting heavily and falling back on the bed.

I didn't respond; I just smirked and headed to the bathroom to grab a washcloth to clean us up with. Once I was done, I slid on my robe and walked back into the bedroom.

"So, what's the deal wit that lil shit I put you on?" he asked me.

"The shit is not goin according to plan at all; them niggas don't fuckin trust me." I replied, sucking my teeth.

"But I thought you said yo cousin fuck wit Gotti," he asked.

"She does, but that nigga don't fuck wit me at all and he damn sure ain't bout to let me know where he stays."

"Well, all I know is that muthafucka hit my traps and then had the nerve to tell them to let me know who did it. He's a bold son of a bitch, I give him that!" Tamir argued heatedly.

Yea, I know what you thinking, I'm a grimy bitch for fuckin wit the enemy, right? I don't give a fuck; Tamir wasn't *my* enemy.

Plus, the nigga had some dope dick. I wanted Gotti in the worst way, but he wouldn't give me the time of day. Instead, he wanted a basic bitch like Azuri.

Don't get me wrong. I had love for my cousin, but not like that and I really didn't like the bitch. Yea, she had it rough, but that bitch always came out on top; hell, she pulled the biggest baller in NY while her ass was working at McDonald's. Some may call me a hater, but that's not the case. I had eyes on Gotti first and her ass should've known better.

I tried him on more than one occasion, but that nigga shut me down at every turn. So, when Tamir approached me a lil while back, I said fuck it. I could get me some good dick, make some money, and get revenge at the same damn time; that shit sounded like a plan to me.

I couldn't tell you why I was the way that I was. Shit, I had a great childhood and even though my father wasn't around, my mother made sure I didn't want for shit. I guess I just didn't give a fuck about nobody but Naomi and wasn't shit wrong with that. I didn't do love; shit, money was the motivation and that shit could make me cum like no other. I wasn't into the kids, white picket fence, and that other bullshit, just give me the money and I would be straight.

"You need to find a way for them niggas to trust you. I tried to hit that nigga other traps, but he changed shit up and moved every fuckin thing. I just need you to find out where that nigga lay his head at, so I can get at his ass," Tamir said, pulling his jeans on.

"You leaving?"

"Yea, I got moves to make and yo ass do too," he told me.

Slightly rolling my eyes, I watched in silence as he got dressed. Tamir was a fine ass nigga and tatted the fuck up just like I liked em. Standing at six feet even, a toffee colored complexion, dark brown eyes framed by the curliest set of eyelashes known to man. His curly tapered fro was neatly cut and soft to the touch. Succulent lips surrounded by a neatly trimmed goatee, the nigga was fine; he kind of reminded me of Mendeecees from Love and Hip Hop.

"Take care of that shit Nay. The next time I come through here, yo ass better have some info for me," he said before walking out the door.

I sat there thinking about what happened the night before. I was still in disbelief that none of them would bring me home. Then, on top of that, I had to take a fuckin Uber. To make matters worse, Azuri let the shit happen and that really pissed me the fuck off. Granted, I had left her hanging a time or two, but still.

Grabbing my phone, I logged onto Facebook and scrolled through my timeline before posting a status about how you couldn't trust people, especially family. I knew the moment Azuri saw it, she would call me and I was gonna play on that shit.

Ten minutes later, just like clockwork, she was calling. I made sure to throw hella shade her way and give her nothing but attitude. The conversation was working until Gotti snatched the phone. I damn near came from the sound of his smooth voice. He talked shit, as usual, before hanging up on my ass.

Gotti was the king of assholes, but the nigga was fine as fuck and paid out the ass. My phone ringing snapped me out of my thoughts.

"What's up bitch?" I asked Zena.

"Shit, what you got goin on?"

Yea, Zena was my girl and I knew that she was gonna run up on Azuri that day in the store. Who do you think told her where we were going to be? I thought that the fight between the two and the things that Zena said would be enough for her to back away from Gotti, but that wasn't the case.

"You comin out today?"

"Yea, I'm gettin dressed right now," I told her.

"Well, come through," she replied.

"I'll call you when I'm on my way," I said before ending the call.

While I was getting dressed, I tried to think of ways to get Gotti on my good side, but I couldn't come up with shit. I couldn't use my pussy, cause that nigga wasn't biting; I didn't know what the fuck to do. I even tried to get at Jahzir, but he was just as bad as Gotti. I mean, I knew my name was ringing bells in the streets, but I didn't give a fuck.

But that didn't give them the right to disrespect me the way they did. The only one that gave me the slightest respect was Dru and just like that, a lightbulb went off in my head. I would use Dru to get inside the circle; shit, he was sexy and getting money, so it wouldn't be too bad.

Smiling to myself, I continued to get dressed and formulate my plan in my head. The only downside to my plan failing was getting caught because these niggas were ruthless, but I couldn't think about that shit right now. I was on a paper chase and I didn't give a fuck who I had to hurt in the process.

Chapter 27: Gotti

It had been a month since shit went down in Philly and that nigga Tamir had been quiet, but I knew he was somewhere plotting. I didn't give a fuck what he had planned, cause I was ready for whatever. The nigga was gon die though, wasn't no way around that shit; he violated and fucked wit the wrong one.

I knew he was gon try to retaliate, so me and Jah switched all our traps around. If it was one thing I didn't play about, it was my money. I kept trying to rack my brain and figure out why the nigga was coming at me so hard. He had a good lil operation going on in Philly, so what the fuck he wanted with mine, I didn't know.

"Kashy, what do you think about me going back to school?" Azuri asked, snapping me out of my thoughts.

"If that's what you wanna do ma, you know I'm behind you a thousand percent," I told her, rubbing her feet.

We were having a Netflix and chill day, even though we were barely paying attention to the movie.

"What you wanna go for?" I asked, sparking up a blunt.

"I don't know yet, but I'll figure it out." She shrugged.

"How you like workin wit my dukes?" I asked her, passing the blunt.

"I love it! The employees are chill and do their job, so I really don't have to do much, except the paperwork."

I nodded my head and listened to her talk while staring at her. She was so fuckin beautiful and she was all mine. A nigga never saw himself falling in love, but I couldn't imagine a life without Azuri in it; that girl was my world.

"Why you starin at me like that?" she asked, snapping me out of my thoughts of her.

"Cause I think you the prettiest girl in the world." I grinned.

"You so full of shit," she giggled.

"Real talk Stink, I love yo melanin girl," I told her.

She blushed slightly and I pulled her onto my lap, continuing to stare at her pretty ass. Even though it had only been about six months, I knew that she was it for me. I hadn't even fucked wit any other bitches since I started fuckin with her.

"Blow me a shotgun ma," I told her.

She pulled on the blunt and sexily blew the smoke into my mouth. Inhaling the smoke, I blew it back into her mouth before kissing her juicy lips.

"You gon marry me Stink?" I asked, looking into her eyes.

"Huh?" she asked with wide eyes.

"You heard me, ma; you gon marry a nigga one day?"

"You sure you could be with just me for the rest of your life?"

"Hell yea! You fine as fuck, can cook yo ass off, and the pussy platinum; my ass ain't goin no got damn where!" I told her seriously.

She went into a fit of giggles, that's how I knew her ass was high as fuck.

"Hmmm, I don't know, I gotta explore the rest of my options," she joked.

I didn't see a got damn thing funny though.

"Don't fuck around and get somebody innocent killed Stink," I said with fire in my eyes.

"I'm just playin bae." She laughed.

"Don't play like that Stink, I'll burn down a whole fuckin city behind yo ass," I replied.

I don't know why, but the shit she said to a nigga had me hot a lil bit. I mean, I knew she was just playing but still. I didn't want to even think about my bitch fuckin wit somebody else; the thought alone was enough to send me over the edge.

"You know I don't see nobody but you bae; it ain't shit another nigga could offer me, cause I ain't goin nowhere," she said, getting serious.

I cracked a small smile when she said that shit, then kissed her lips softly.

"You still ain't answer my question," I smirked.

"Of course I'm gonna marry you someday," she replied, playfully rolling her eyes.

"And you gon give me five bad ass kids," I added.

"Who pushing out five babies?" she asked, looking at me like I had lost my mind.

"That fuckin owl, the fuck you think," I replied, turning my face up.

"I'm not having five babies Kashmir, more like two," she said.

"Yea aight ma, we'll see." I waved.

"Shit, I'm surprised yo ass ain't pregnant now, the way I been up in that thang." I grinned.

"Birth control baby," she smirked.

"Yea, I'm gon need for you to get off that shit like asap," I told her.

"I'm not ready for kids Kashmir," she confessed.

"Shit, well yo ass better get ready." I shrugged.

"You can't bully me into having kids," she said, folding her arms.

"I ain't gotta bully you into shit; I just don't want to be old as fuck when I start having kids. A nigga right around the corner from thirty and I want me some bad ass kids running around here; plus, my dukes want some grandkids."

"So, I just ain't got no say so in this shit, huh?" she asked.

"Nah, not really," I smirked.

She sucked her teeth and climbed off my lap, pulling the shorts out her ass. I smacked her ass hard, just to watch it jiggle, and she mushed me before walking out the room. I started to go behind her, but my phone ringing stopped me.

"Yo!"

"What's good big bro?" Jah asked.

"Ain't shit, playin the crib today, tryin to get Azuri pregnant and shit." I laughed, even though I was serious.

"You hell man, but I called to tell yo ass that Megan ol apple ass head pregnant and shit," he told me.

"Word? That's what's up man, congrats!"

"Hell yea, a nigga excited man and you already know I had to call you first."

"Damn son, my baby brother havin a baby before my ass, ain't that some shit." I laughed.

"Nigga, yo ass wasn't tryin to have no babies by none of these hoes out here no way." He laughed.

"True story, but I done found my wife, so it's a wrap!"

"Who the fuck are you and what yo ass do wit Gotti, nigga talkin bout marriage and shit," he joked.

"Fuck you, nigga! Shit, yo ass basically married too, so kiss my ass!"

"Man, ain't nobody gon marry Megan ol big head ass," he joked.

"Don't get fucked up Jah!" I heard Megan shout.

"Go head on girl." He laughed.

"Nigga, handle that shit and call me back," I told him.

"Aight bruh," he said, hanging up.

Taking the stairs two at a time, I headed to my bedroom and saw Azuri laid across the bed reading.

"How you posed to be chillin wit ya nigga and you up here reading?" I asked, climbing on top of her.

"You were on the phone," she giggled.

I kissed her soft lips and took the kindle out her hand.

"Megan havin a baby and shit," I told her.

"Duh, I been knew that." She laughed.

"That mean you next," I replied.

"Kashy," she whined.

"Shut the fuck up," I said before sticking my tongue down her throat.

For the rest of the day, I made love to my girl and made sure to empty my seed into her. I knew that she didn't take her pill today because I peeped the pack on the dresser and the pill for today was still in there. I could only hope I got her ass pregnant. I didn't know why I was so hell bent on her having my seed, but I was, and that shit was gon happen. I didn't give a fuck what she had to say about it.

Hours later, after we were both drained and sleep, the phone rang, waking us both up.

"Yo!" I answered groggily.

"Kashmir, oh God!" Megan cried.

Sitting straight up in the bed, my heart raced as her cries filled the phone.

"Megan, what happened sis?" I asked her.

"He… they… oh God Kashmir! They shot him!" she screamed.

"Shot who?" I asked, standing up from the bed; a sinking feeling hit me in my gut.

"Jahzir! I can't lose him Gotti, I just can't!"

My knees damn near buckled when she said that shit and my heart beat out of my fucking chest. Rage filled my body and tears filled my eyes.

"What hospital?"

"Bellevue, please get here Gotti," she cried softly before wailing loudly.

Her cries did something to me, so I just ended the call before rushing to get dressed.

"What's wrong Kashy?" Azuri asked, standing by my side.

"Jah got shot," I told her.

"Oh my God," she said, covering her mouth with tears in her eyes.

We both quickly got dressed and headed to Bellevue, praying that my brother was ok. I know that say men ain't supposed to cry, but as soon as I pulled up to the hospital, a nigga broke down. I couldn't lose Jah, not my little brother; that nigga was everything to me and I wouldn't make it without him.

"Let it out baby," Azuri said, rubbing my back soothingly. "He's gonna be ok, we just gotta have faith," she told me, while wiping my tears.

I held onto her for dear life as we cried together. Finally, getting ourselves together, we got out the truck and headed inside the hospital. I spotted Megan, my parents, and my crew immediately.

"What happened?" I asked, hugging Megan tightly.

I knew that she had to be with him because her cream dress and hands were covered in blood.

"We went out to dinner, you know, to celebrate the baby and everything. Just as we were leaving, Azuri, your cousin Naomi came in with some dude we had never seen before. He looked at Jah and smirked; a bad feeling rushed through me, so I ushered Jah out the door. While we were waiting for the valet to bring the car around, a car came up and they just opened fire. Jah pulled me down to the ground, then started shooting back. He collapsed beside me, I couldn't even tell how many times he had been shot. There was just so much blood Gotti," she cried.

I hugged her tightly and allowed her to cry. My father looked at me with murder in his eyes, silently letting me know that he was coming out of retirement. I nodded my head, letting him know that I understood.

We sat around for the next two hours on pins and needles. Just when I was about to act ignorant, a doctor came from the back.

"Family of Jahzir Banks?" he asked.

"That's my son and this is his wife, how is he?" my dad asked.

"Well, Mr. Banks was hit a total of five times. Four went through and through, the fifth one had to be removed surgically; it also punctured his left lung. We lost him twice, but we were able to get him back. He had to be placed on a ventilator because he's not breathing on his own. The next twenty-four hours are very critical for Mr. Banks and there is a chance that he will not make it through the night. We're gonna monitor him and if he does make it, we'll do a cat scan to ensure that he still has brain activity," he explained sympathetically.

The only thing I heard was that my brother may not make it through the night and a nigga fuckin lost it. My pops and Dru grabbed me, dragging me out of the hospital as a nigga went ballistic.

I stared at Azuri with murder in my eyes.

"Yo hoe ass cousin is dead if she had anything to do with this shit and that's on God!" I shouted, meaning every single word before they pulled me out the hospital.

Chapter 28: Azuri

I stood at a loss for words as I watched Kashmir's father and his boys push him out the doors. Megan was over in the corner crying her eyes out, while Gina showed her support. I wanted to comfort her but I couldn't move. The last words Kashmir spoke to me kept echoing in my head. His words were deadly and laced with conviction. At this point, I didn't know how to feel but I knew I wanted to get out of here.

"Gina, I'm about to leave. I don't feel like this is the place for me right now. Megan, I will call and check on you, boo. Just try to think positive and keep your head up. Jahzir is going to pull through; he's a fighter."

"Azuri, you don't have to leave baby," Gina said.

"I know but I think its best."

I gave them both a hug then walked towards the doors, trying to hold back the tears that were trying to fall from my eyes. Kashmir had the keys to the truck, so I was just going to catch a cab. I knew he was hurting and I didn't want to bother him.

"Where the fuck you think you're going Azuri?" his voice caused me to freeze in mid stride in the middle of the parking lot. I slowly turned around to only be met by Gotti because this damn sure wasn't Kashy.

"I thought it would be best if I leave-" I tried to explain but he cut me off.

"This is the bullshit yo ass is really trying to do right now. My brother is laid up in the hospital fighting for his life and you trying to leave? The fuck kind of shit are you on Azuri!"

"What else do you want me to do? You just fucking told me how you were going to kill my fucking cousin Kashmir."

"The bitch is foul; I don't know how many different ways I have to tell you that shit. I'm starting to think yo ass is fucking dumb. You heard what the fuck Megan said. Your cousin had something to do with this shit, so she's gonna get handled."

"You don't know Naomi had something to do with this. Megan said she saw my cousin with a dude she never seen before. She never said my cousin pulled the trigger or some shit."

If looks could kill, my ass would be on the ground struggling for air from the way Kashmir stared at me. He inched closer to me and I tried backing up, but he stopped me by grabbing the front of my shirt.

"Kashmir, let me go," I whined, trying to fight him off.

"Shut the fuck up. You defending that bitch like you know something that I don't Azuri. The fuck do you know?" he gritted.

"I don't know anything. I was at home just like you were."

"That don't mean shit. You don't even rock with yo cousin like that but you defending her. That shit makes you look real suspect."

"Really Kashmir, you're going to fucking go there nigga." I understood Kashmir was in his feelings behind his brother; however, this nigga was taking shit a little too far.

"You fucking right that's where I'm going with this shit. You defending this bitch and you don't even like her hoe ass. That shit is all starting to make sense now." He pushed me away, causing me to fall off balance a little.

"Gotti, chill the fuck out. I didn't raise you to be putting your hands on woman," his pops said, rushing over to where we were.

"Pops, no disrespect, but mind yo business. This has to do with me and Zuri," Kashmir said, grilling his father. I was taken back by his whole attitude.

"It became my business the minute you put your hands on this girl. I understand you're hurting but you will not disrespect Azuri in my presence."

Kashmir looked at his father before walking off towards the truck. He got in and pulled off, never giving me a second look. I sighed because everything got out of hand so quickly.

"Azuri, don't worry 'bout him. He's just hurting."

"I know," I whispered.

I said my goodbyes then called an Uber to take me to my aunt's house. Naomi and I wasn't close but I would like to think I knew my cousin. There wasn't no way her ass could have something to do with Jazhir getting shot. I just couldn't picture Naomi being that dumb. If she did have something to do with it, then I didn't know how the hell she was going to get herself out of this one. Kashmir was out for blood and her dumb ass was the first person on his list.

* * * *

"Azuri, what are you doing over here?" my mother asked when I walked inside my aunt's house.

"I came over here to talk to Naomi about something. Hey auntie, where's Naomi?"

"You're asking the wrong person. I know that's my daughter and shit, but she is the hardest person to keep up with. She switches dudes like she switches her panties," my aunt said, shaking her head.

"Let me call her and find out where she is."

I pulled my phone to call her but she beat me to it. Before I could even dial a number, Naomi's name was flashing on my home screen.

"Naomi, where are you; we need to talk like yesterday?" There was no need for a pleasant greeting because our conversation wasn't going to be pleasant at all.

"Meet me at my mom's house. I should be there in the next five minutes."

"I'm already here. My mom is here too, so I'll meet you outside." I hung up the phone and looked back towards my mother and aunt.

"She's about to pull up now. I'ma wait for her outside."

I walked out the house and the block was hot but that shit wasn't nothing new. It was summer time and everyone was trying to show out. I sat on the stoop outside of my aunt's house, impatiently waiting for Naomi. I was bouncing my knee saying a silent prayer that Kashmir was wrong about Naomi because if he was right, it was about to be some shit. Nine times out of ten, I would have to choose and that was something I wasn't willing to do. At the end of the day, Naomi was still family; then, on the other hand, Kashmir was the love of my life. How could I choose between the two of them? I tried to shake the thoughts because there was no use in thinking about that when I didn't know the truth yet.

Five minutes turned to ten and ten turned to fifteen minutes when Naomi finally pulled up. She got out of a black Mercedes Benz, along with a dude I never seen before. I guess this was the same dude Megan had seen her with when they went to the restaurant.

"Nice of you to finally show up Ms. I'm five minutes away."

"No need for the sass Azuri. Mir, this is Azuri and Azuri, this is Mir," she said, rolling her eyes. "Baby, let me talk to my cousin right quick and then we can go," she said to the dude. The dude she was with wasn't paying her ass any mind because he was eye fucking the shit out of me. His eyes roamed my body as his tongue glided across his lips.

"Do you mind keeping your eyes to yourself?" I asked him.

"Azuri, what are you talking about?" Naomi questioned.

"Naomi, don't be stupid. You are over here talking to this dude and instead of him listening to what you have to say, he's over here eye fucking the shit out of me."

"Azuri everyone doesn't want you-" Naomi began but the dude cut her off.

"Yeah, I was eye fucking you and what. The fuck you gonna do shawty?" he questioned, getting closer to me.

"Naomi, get your nigga," I told her, taking a couple of steps back.

"I don't belong to Naomi, so she won't be getting this nigga."

"Really Mir, that's how we giving it up?" Naomi asked, looking pissed off.

"Naomi, don't try that dumb shit; you already know what it is" He looked back at Naomi then returned his attention back to me.

"So, wassup Azuri. You gonna let me get to know you and spend some time." His hand caressed my face and I slapped it away.

"Nigga, don't touch my face. Naomi, get this dude because he's being straight disrespectful and you know we don't even do that type of thing. Plus, my time is already occupied. Naomi, can we talk please?" I stressed the word please because I really wanted to get this conversation over, so I could go about my business.

"Yeah," Naomi said, looking between her dude and I. "Mir, I'll be right back."

Naomi walked around Mir and pulled me over to the side. Mir laughed, then got back in his car.

"Azuri, you need to stop flirting with my man because that shit is disrespectful to me and Gotti," was the first thing out of Naomi's mouth. I looked at her as if she was stupid.

"Naomi, what the hell are you talking about? Nobody was flirting with that nigga. If anyone was doing the flirting, it was him. So, you can take all that misdirected anger and push it in his direction. I don't even know why you are defending that nigga when he obviously said that the two of y'all aren't together."

"Don't worry about the two of us being together; worry about your own nigga. The streets are talking and they saying his time on this green earth is limited."

"Is that the streets talking or is that you talking Naomi?"

"It's the streets talking. Gotti isn't the only nigga in town making big moves."

"Mhmm, that's really interesting for you to say. You know Jahzir got shot?"

"I heard about that too. It's sad because I planned on making him my baby daddy," Naomi said, shaking her head.

"Naomi, did you have anything to do with it?" I just threw the question out there because there was no need on beating around the bush.

"Why would you think I had something to do with it?" she asked with a hint of laughter in her voice.

"Because you are a shady fucking individual. Stop playing games and just tell me if you did the shit or not. I'm trying to save your fucking life."

She started laughing, as if something was really funny. "Save my life from who, Gotti. Nobody is scared of that nigga Azuri, besides you. Gotti walking around with a death sentence. You're my family, so of course I'm going to warn you; that was the point of me calling you today. You need to leave that nigga alone before you get caught up in the cross fire."

Hearing her talk about Kashmir being a dead man did something to me. All I was seeing was red when I pounced on her ass. We were going blow for blow, but I wouldn't be satisfied until her ass blacked out. Just when I got her ass on the ground, I felt a pair of strong arms pulling me off. I knew it wasn't Kashmir, so I tried to fight the nigga off.

"Chill the fuck out mama. If you fuck me up, I might have to change my mind about making you my wife."

Mir carried me over to his truck while I was still trying to beat his ass. He sat me on the hood of it and backed up a little. I jumped off the hood and close enough to him, smacking the shit out of him.

"Don't you ever put your fucking hands on me again. Instead of trying to pull me off your girlfriend, you need to be going to help that bitch up," I ranted. My chest was heaving up and down.

"Ma, you feisty as fuck." He smiled, pulling me around the waist then laying his lips against mine. I was caught off guard and my body was frozen until I heard the voice of the grim reaper himself.

"Nigga, didn't yo mother ever tell you not to touch shit that doesn't belong to you." Kashmir's icy tone was followed up by the cocking of a gun.

Chapter 29: Gotti

The argument I had with Azuri wasn't sitting well with me. I blanked on her for no reason and a nigga was feeling real fucked up about it. When I left the hospital, I drove around for a while, trying to will myself to calm down before I did something stupid. I tried calling Azuri, but her phone was going straight to voicemail.

Just when I was about to call her again, a call from Nala came through.

"What's up Ma?"

"Kashmir, get over here before Azuri kills this girl!" she shouted.

"Who?" I asked in confusion.

"Naomi!"

I quickly busted an illegal U-turn and sped to Azuri's aunt's crib. My knuckles were turning white; I was gripping the steering wheel so tight. Pulling up, I saw a nigga I didn't know with his hands on something that didn't belong to him. The fuck nigga then crossed the line by putting his lips on what was mine.

Slamming on brakes, I grabbed my gun and hopped out with the quickness.

"Nigga, didn't yo mother ever tell you not to touch shit that doesn't belong to you," I spoke in a tone that could've frozen hell over.

Azuri froze in fear, but this cocky bastard just turned around and smirked.

"Well, well, well, if it isn't the infamous Gotti." He laughed.

"Yo, my nigga, I need for you to get yo fuckin hands off my wife. Since you spoke my name, I'm sure that you know my reputation and you know how the fuck I get down. Bring yo ass over here Stink!"

Azuri looked between us hesitantly, as if she didn't know what to do and it was then that I saw this nigga had a gun pointed in her side.

"Nah, my nigga, *Stink* is goin with me and it ain't shit you can do about it! Naomi, come over here and open this door!" he barked.

I chuckled lightly, even though wasn't shit funny, but I needed to calm the rage that was flowing through my body.

"Nigga, you crazy as fuck if you think I'm just gon stand here and let you take my bitch! Naomi, I swear to God if you take one muthafuckin step, yo mama will be burying yo funky ass!" I threatened.

"What the hell is goin on out here?" Violet asked, rushing down the stairs with Nala behind her.

"Ask your hoe ass daughter," I spat, never taking my eyes off Azuri.

She was scared; I saw it in her eyes, but I gave her a reassuring wink that everything was gonna be ok.

"Look muthafucka, it's obvious that yo beef is with me, so let my girl go and we can handle shit," I said, trying to compromise.

"You know, for you to be so smart, you a dumb muthafucka. You couldn't possibly think that after you came to Philly and did the shit you did, that I wouldn't come after you," he replied.

It was then that it registered to me, this was Tamir. I had never seen the nigga before today, so I didn't know who he was.

"So, you the nigga that wanna be me?" I laughed.

"Newsflash muthafucka, you could never be me, even on my worst day. You're an amateur and I'm in the majors. I like to think I'm a fair man though, so I'll give you a few options. Option number one, let my girl go and get as far away from my city as possible and I might let you live. Option number two, I can have yo whole family killed in a matter of seconds with one phone call, even your precious wife and three daughters."

His eyes grew wide with that revelation; nigga didn't think nobody knew about them. Nigga out here trickin off on Naomi's hoe ass and had a whole fucking family in Philly. My team was thorough with their research, so it wasn't much I didn't know about Tamir Hall. The nigga was gonna die regardless though and I'm sure he knew that.

"What's it gonna be, my nigga? You want Tamia, Tamira, and Tanaya's blood on your hands?" I asked, smiling evilly after naming his daughters.

I knew the nigga was a fuck nigga when he had to think about it. He decided to make the right choice and pushed Azuri toward me.

"I'll see you again, my nigga!" he threatened.

"I'll be waitin pussy!" I spat.

He hopped in his truck accompanied by Naomi and they sped off. Shaking my head, I put my gun in my waist and pulled Azuri into me. Hugging her tightly, I buried my face in her neck inhaling her scent and just like that, I was calm again.

Some of y'all might think I'm crazy for letting him go, but there was always a method to my madness. Trust and believe, Tamir was gonna get his, but I had to make sure my baby was good first. Unbeknownst to him, there was somebody close to his ass that hated the very ground he walked on and wanted him dead just as much as I did.

"You ok ma?" I asked her.

"I'm better now, I don't know what would've happened if you didn't show up," she cried.

"Shh, don't cry Stink, I told you that I would always protect you, ma," I told her, wiping her tears.

"I don't like this shit not one bit! Now Violet, you're my sister and Naomi is my niece, but her little ass needs a reality check."

"I just don't know where I went wrong with that girl and for her to actually leave with that nigga," Violet said, shaking her head.

I didn't comment because Naomi was gonna die and that was all there was to it. She made her decision the moment she got in the truck with that fuck nigga.

"Can you please take me home?" Azuri asked softly.

Nodding my head, I helped her in the car, then talked to Nala for a minute. She asked me to drop her off at the hospital, so she could sit with my mother. I nodded my head and hopped in the truck.

The car ride was silent, everybody lost in their own thoughts. My mind drifted to my little brother and a nigga teared up a lil bit. Jahzir was more than my brother; he was my best friend and the right to my left. I didn't know what I would do if he didn't make it, but I did know that I would never be the same.

"Let my mom know that I'll be back up here later, but make sure to call me if there are any changes," I told Nala, as we pulled up to the hospital.

"Ok baby, just pray," she said, giving me a small smile before climbing out the car.

Thirty minutes later, we were pulling up to my house. I killed the ignition and sighed heavily. Azuri climbed out the car and I told her I would be in shortly. As soon as she closed the door, I lit a blunt and reclined in my seat. For some reason, I felt like Jah was already gone and that shit hit a nigga hard.

You know how they say siblings have that kind of bond that you can feel each other? Well, that shit was true and right now, I didn't feel Jah at all. Silent tears rolled down my face as I smoked my blunt and remembered the crazy ass times I had with Jah.

* * * *

"You ready?" Azuri asked me.

I sighed deeply before placing my dark Gucci shades over my eyes. Looking up at the church, my heart pounded up against my chest. How the fuck did we end up here? Shit wasn't supposed to happen this way.

"Nah, I ain't ready, but I ain't got no choice but to be," I replied before sliding out the car and grabbing her hand.

Megan grabbed my other hand and held onto it for dear life. Entering the packed church, my eyes focused on the black casket that sat at the front. I felt Megan tremble slightly, so I wrapped my arm around her and pulled her close. The walk to the front seemed so long, tears blurred my vision, but I swallowed them down.

Finally making our way to the front, I stared down at my baby brother. My nigga looked good, decked down in a white Armani suit, but this shit didn't even feel right. I wasn't supposed to bury my little brother; he was supposed to bury me. Our whole life I protected him and now I felt as if I failed him.

"Jahhhhhhhh!" Megan screamed, collapsing up against me.

I let Azuri's hand go and wrapped both arms around Megan, holding her tightly as she cried. The gut wrenching scream from my mother caused the tears I so desperately tried to hold to come rushing out of my eyes.

Breaking free from my grasp, Megan placed her hands on Jah's chest and begged him to come back to her. Planting kisses on his cold face as she cried, the scene was too much for me to handle. Azuri rubbed her back, while trying to keep herself together. It took me and my pop to get Megan to her seat.

Once we were seated, I pulled both Megan and Azuri into me, then the service began. The shit went by in a big ass blur. I kept praying that this was all a dream and that I would wake up at any moment, but it never happened.

Pictures of Jah played out on a jumbo Tron, while people came up to pay their respects. Jah had definitely brought the city out cause everybody came to show my nigga love; there wasn't a seat left and a lot of people were standing up. The preacher preached a bunch of bullshit because he didn't know my brother from a can of paint. A few people sang and before I knew it, the service was over and we were headed to the cemetery.

"Ashes to ashes, dust to dust, rest well brother Jahzir..." the preacher spoke before praying.

They gave us a chance to say our final goodbyes, so we gathered around the casket and took turns kissing Jah goodbye. My mother damn near passed out, so my father had to pull her away. Nala sat next to her and held her as she cried. My pops tried to keep it together, but even he dropped some tears. Azuri kissed his cheek and told him that she loved him as she cried.

Before I knew it, it was my turn. I stared at him for a while and he just looked as if he was sleeping.

"Look out for me, lil bro, cause a nigga bout to go on a warpath," I whispered in his ear before kissing his forehead.

Megan grabbed onto him and wouldn't let go as she lost it, along with my mother, who was sobbing loudly. Once we got her together, they closed the casket back.

The funeral director gave the go ahead and the casket slowly descended into the ground. Megan fell to her knees and screamed for them to pull him up. My father grabbed her, in fear that she might actually try to jump inside the hole.

They handed me a shovel and with tear filled eyes, I tossed the first shovel full of dirt onto Jah's casket. I handed it to my father and watched as he did the same.

The crowd dispersed, but I remained staring down into the hole that had become my brother's final resting place. Taking a seat on the ground, I put my head down and let out an animalistic wail, finally breaking down.

"This shit ain't right Jah," I repeated over and over again. "I'm sorry Jah man, I'm so fuckin sorry bruh," I cried.

I smelled Azuri before I felt her presence; she sat down next to me and wrapped her arms around me, pulling me into her chest.

"Why ma? Why the fuck did my brother have to die?" I asked her, even though I knew she didn't have the answers I was so desperately searching for.

"I don't know Kashy, only God does," she replied softly.

For close to an hour, Azuri held me as I cried for my little brother. Once I was done, a nigga felt drained, but the rage that flowed through my veins was undeniable.

Pulling away from Azuri, I stood up and with one last glance at the grave, I walked away.

"Lord, forgive me for the havoc I'm about to wreak and Jah, I'm sorry," I spoke.

Chapter 30: Azuri

Since Jahzir's death, everyone seemed to be just going through life without a purpose. It's been a couple of weeks since the funeral and it was as if everyone's spirit was buried with Jahzir. Gina and I didn't work together as much anymore; she barely even came into work. When I would talk to my mother about it, she would just say that this was Gina's grieving process. I couldn't complain because everyone grieved in their own way. I just wished everyone would pull their selves together a little. Kashmir was in and out of the house all the time, leaving me alone once again. The only difference was he would text me through the day to make sure I was straight and to let me know that he was good.

Other than that, life has been life. Naomi was still MIA with ole boy. I couldn't believe that bitch and when I saw her again, she was getting that ass beat once more. I was having conflicted feelings because I felt Naomi deserved everything that was coming her way, but at the same time, I didn't think my aunt deserved to go through the same pain Gina had to go through. I haven't voiced my opinion to Kashmir because that was only an argument waiting to happen. I didn't know when but at some point, I was gonna have to talk to him about the situation.

Since today was my early day at work, I was going to go food shopping to pick up a couple of things to make dinner for Kashmir. I felt we needed to have an intimate moment or something.

"Azuri, a chick is out here asking for the manager. She's trying to return a pair of shoes that she obviously wore," Brydell said, coming into the office.

"Okay, tell her I will be out in a minute." Brydell left the office and I sat there for a second, pulling myself together because it was about to be some shit.

After gathering myself, I walked out to the front looking for the lady who had an issue. It wasn't hard to find her because she was grilling me as I was grilling her.

"Zena, what are you doing here?"

"Look who down moved on up in the world." She laughed, walking over to me. I bit my bottom lip, trying to remind myself that I needed to be professional.

"Zena, I will ask you again, what are you doing here?"

"What does it look like I'm doing here? I know that little bitch done told you that I'm trying to exchange these shoes. So, instead of playing dumb, go behind the register and give me my schmoney."

"What you're not going to do is come in here and be disrespectful. If you want help with something, then I advise you to fix that fucked up attitude you got going on."

"I don't need to fix shit. Just return my shoes," she spat.

I snatched the box out her hand to get a look at the shoes she was trying to return. Opening the box, a blind person could tell that she had worn these shoes. The heel was broken in and the bottom of one shoe had gum on it.

"Zena, you can't be serious. I'm not returning these shoes because you shouldn't have brought them if you couldn't afford them."

"Like hell you won't return them." I was happy there wasn't that many customers in the shop because with the way Zena was acting, we would have lost a few sales.

"Zena, it is apparent that you wore these shoes to the club. I'm not returning them, the door is over there, and you can have a nice day."

"Bitch, don't tell me to have no fucking nice day. Now, it's either you are going to return these shoes or I'm taking another pair."

I chuckled softly because this bitch was really testing me right now. I sat the box of shoes on the counter behind me, then took a hold of Zena's arm. She tried to snatch it away from me, but I had the death grip on it. I dragged her ass outside of the store as she was screaming and yelling a whole bunch of nonsense. When we got outside, I pushed her.

"Zena, get the fuck away from my store before I beat that ass again."

"Try me bitch!" She stepped towards me, dropping her bag on the floor.

"You just don't learn-"

"Azuri, the fuck you out here doing?" Out of nowhere, Kashmir walked up stepping in between Zena and I, giving her his back.

"Kashmir, where did you come from?" I questioned.

"It doesn't matter where I came from. Yo ass supposed to be working, not fighting irrelevant bitches."

"Was I irrelevant when I was sucking yo dick?" Zena sassed from behind me.

"Matter of fact, you were and yo ass is still fucking irrelevant. Zena, I been feeling real trigger happy lately," he said it to her but was staring at me.

I went to look around him and her ass was gone that fucking fast. I shook my head because the bitch only had mouth when Kashmir wasn't around.

"Stink, the fuck was you doing out here?"

"I escorted her out of the store then she wanted to fight me. What was I supposed to just let her beat my ass?"

"Of course you not gonna let her beat your ass but from the looks of shit, you were about to throw the first punch. I already have enough shit going on, I don't need you out in here fighting and shit over petty stuff."

"I hear you Kashy, but-"

"But nothing Stink! You have to learn when to pick and choose your battles; it's as simple as that." Without even allowing me to say another word, he just walked off.

If I didn't have to work, I would've ran after him but duty calls. I went back in the store and assisted Brydell with the remaining of the customers. A whole half an hour later, Kashmir came back to the store with two bouquets of pink roses.

"Come in the back Stink." I told Brydell to hold down the floor and followed Kashmir to the back.

"Are these for me?" I questioned.

"Yeah, who else am I bringing flowers too, Zuri," he said sarcastically.

"No need for all of that, smart ass." I took one of the bouquets and smelled it. The smell was lovely and for some odd reason, it warmed my heart.

"You like them?" he asked.

"I love them baby, thank you."

"Good Azuri, I want to talk about something with you." He sounded serious as hell. I took my bouquet and sat on the desk, waiting for him to say whatever he needed to say.

"Stink, on the real, I been thinking about life a lot these past couple of weeks. None of this shit we got going on is a guarantee. Life isn't even fucking promised. I can walk out of here today and be dead in five minutes. That's how real this shit is."

"Kashy, what are you talking about? You're scaring me a little."

"All I'm trying to say is that people put time limits on when to fall in love and when to get married, when we don't even know if we are gonna be here tomorrow and shit. I don't want to be like them people. I fell in love with you when you ripped up that hundred and threw the shit at me. I may not have known it then, but I know it now. All I see is you, ma, and everything has been 'bout you since we first started kicking it. I don't sleep right knowing Azuri isn't followed by Banks."

"Uh Kashmir, what are you trying to say?" I prayed like hell he wasn't saying what I thought he was saying.

"I'm saying you gonna help a nigga sleep good at night by adorning his last name."

Kashmir went into his pocket, pulling out a little black box. He went to open it and I quickly reached my hand out, placing it on top of his so he wouldn't open the box.

"Kashmir, we can't," I whispered.

"Come again Stink?" he asked with a raised eye brow.

"Kashmir, we can't do this," I repeated.

"Why the fuck we can't do this Azuri? You love me right?" his voice echoed throughout the office, causing whatever words that were supposed to come out my mouth disappear.

"Don't getting fucking mute now Azuri! Do you fucking love me or don't you?"

"Yes, I love you," I answered.

"Then the fuck you mean we can't do this. Yo, you on your period or some shit?"

"No, I'm not on my period but this isn't really what you want."

"How the fuck are you going to tell me what I want?"

"Because I know you, Kashy. You are grieving the loss of your brother and your scared of losing me. You only think this is what you want but deep down, you know it's not. We have only been dating for months, not years."

"Did you not just hear my fucking speech about people putting time limits on shit? I know what the fuck I want but I'm starting to question what the hell you want."

"Kashmir, don't try and do me like that because I'm being honest with you. If I accept this proposal, it wouldn't be fair to me or you. We still have things that we need to discuss before we get married."

"What do we have to fucking discuss?"

"The whole kid situation. You want them and I'm not ready. Not to mention the thing with Naomi." Now was probably not the right time to address the Naomi situation but it just came out.

"There is nothing to discuss when it comes to Naomi because the bitch is fucking dead."

"I understand she is to blame for Jahzir's death but you just wouldn't be bringing her pain; you will also be bringing my aunt pain. My aunt doesn't deserve to go through the pain of losing the child."

"My mother didn't deserve that shit either! You know what Azuri, you on some straight bullshit, but you did help me realize something."

"Kashmir, calm down; you are being dramatic right now. Let's just go home and talk about this over dinner."

"Nah, I'm good. You were right tho; deep down, I don't want this shit." He got out of the chair he was in and glared at me one last time before walking out the door.

I saw all the hurt and pain was evident in his eyes. I wasn't sure if what I just did was the right thing but it was something that needed to be done. He wasn't looking to marry because of the love he had for me; he wanted to marry me to fill the void of the loss of his brother, his best friend. That void could only be filled with time and healing.

Chapter 31: Gotti

Losing Jahzir was one of the hardest things I've ever had to deal with. It didn't even feel right riding through the city without my brother at my side. A nigga wasn't even really living; I was merely existing and dropping bodies all over the city. Azuri was by my side though, even when I didn't want to be bothered; shorty held me down and I appreciated that shit.

Tamir and Naomi had damn near vanished, but it would only be a matter of time before the two resurfaced, so I really wasn't tripping. I had an inside connect on getting to Tamir, so I knew as soon as they got word on where he was, I would receive a phone call. Until then though, I was gonna continue to fuck up his money.

I had a lot of time to think about shit and I came to the conclusion that, if I was to die soon, I wanted Azuri adorning my last name. If I was being honest, I had been thinking about this shit for months and had my jeweler make her a custom 8 karat diamond halo engagement ring, in a white gold setting.

Nothing in the world had me feeling as fucked up as I did when I left my mother's store. I couldn't wrap my mind around the fact that Azuri turned down my proposal. Then, she gave me some bullshit about me only wanting to marry her so that I didn't lose her. In all the months that we had been together, she still didn't know me.

Kashmir Gotti Banks didn't do shit unless I wanted to. Losing my brother put a lot of shit into perspective for me. Life was short. Shit, you can be gone at any day, so why not give your all to the ones you love? I loved Azuri more than I loved my next breath, but now I was questioning if we should be together or not.

I mean, she fought being with me from day one. I did things for her that I've never done for any female. I needed her like I needed air to breathe, but a part of me didn't feel as if she felt the same way. Then, she spit that dumb shit about her aunt being hurt if something happened to Naomi. But, what about the pain my family felt from losing my brother? It was like that shit didn't even matter to her, so before saying some shit I would regret, I just left. Advice was something I needed, so I went to the one person I knew would give it to me straight with no chaser.

"Hey Ma," I said, kissing her cheek and taking a seat next to her.

Since Jah's passing, she hadn't been the same. Shit, none of us had but my mother especially. She closed herself off and mostly spent her time at home. I didn't think it was healthy, but my pops said it was her grieving process.

"Hey baby," she said, giving me a weak smile.

"How you feeling today?" I asked her.

"Just taking it day by day." She sighed and I nodded my head in agreement.

Silence filled the room, each of us lost in our thoughts. Jahzir filled my mind and I'm sure he filled hers too.

"What's on your mind Kashy?"

"What you mean?"

"You're my son and I know you better than you know yourself, now tell me what happened."

I ran my hand down my face before running down the whole situation with Azuri to her; she sat in silence and just listened.

"Now, don't get upset with me, but I agree with Azuri." I went to object, but she held her hand up.

"Let me finish son. I know you love Azuri, just like I know she loves you, but marriage is a big step; a step that I don't think either one of you are ready to take. If you really want to marry Azuri, marry her because it's what you want deep down in your heart, don't just marry her because you feel like life is short or because you feel like you could die tomorrow. Life was short before Jahzir died and marriage was nowhere on your agenda, so why now? I'll tell you why. You just suffered a traumatic loss, so you're trying to feel that void with Azuri. It doesn't work like that Kashy. Allow yourself to grieve and accept the fact that Jahzir is gone. Right now, your mind is jumbled, so you felt like asking Azuri to marry you was the best thing to do to get your mind off of things. I don't blame her for saying no and you shouldn't either; you're not ready for marriage."

I heard everything she said and I even agreed with some of it, but I also knew that I wanted Azuri to be my wife. Yea, I would say that losing Jah gave me the push I needed to propose, but even if I hadn't lost Jah, I would've proposed to Azuri. I loved that girl and I wasn't too sure she knew how much.

"I hear you, ma, but a part of me feels like maybe it just ain't in the cards for me and Azuri. I didn't say we had to get married tomorrow; I just wanted her to know that I was committed to her and only her. We could've gotten married on her time, I wasn't rushing, I don't know Ma. Since day one, she's been pushing me away, so why should I keep trying? I shouldn't have to keep proving my love to her, either she knows how much I love her or she doesn't. I got too much shit on my plate right now, so maybe this was a sign or some shit." I sighed.

The tightening in my chest at the thought of losing her let me know that it was gonna be hard to let Azuri go, but I felt like this was what was best.

"You don't mean none of what just came out your mouth. You're hurt and that's understandable, but can you really sit here and say that you can live your life without Azuri in it?"

"Nah, I can't," I answered without hesitation. "But if that's what I gotta do, then I will. I can't keep being with somebody that fights me at every turn. Then, for her to ask me to leave Naomi alone knowing damn well that she was partially responsible for Jah's death, that shit don't sit right with me ma," I added.

"Losing a child is something that I don't wish on anybody; the pain and hurt that comes with that is too much to bear. Two wrongs don't make a right though son, sometimes you have to let karma run its course. I'm not sayin that those responsible for Jah's death shouldn't get what's coming to them, but you can't be for certain that Naomi even knew what was about to happen. For all we know, she didn't know shit and was just as shocked as we all were."

I thought about what she was saying and she could've been right, but my gut was telling me that Naomi was smack dab in the middle of this shit.

"Maybe you two should take a step back from each other. Everything with the two of you happened so fast, then with everything that happened in between, it just might be best to get some breathing room," she suggested.

"You might be right ma." I sighed.

"Take the time to grieve for your brother. I know you all worry about me, being that I just sit here and cry sometimes, but it's helping me. We all grieve differently; you just need to figure out a way for Kashmir to grieve."

She gave me a small smile and wiped the tears that fell down her face. I grabbed her hand into mine and kissed the back; she squeezed my hand in response. I sat with my mother for a little while before leaving and going to grab me a pint of Hennessey.

Now look, I couldn't imagine life without you/I just sit

here wonderin why

But the law of life, and god placed us here/And said

everybody must die

Aint it hard trying to move on, but still I try/Even though

we got money, judgement day

Just some things we can't buy/Even though you gone, I

never let you move on

Cause every time I think about you/I sit back and write

your name in a song

Now ashes to ashes, and dust to dirt/It's kinda spooky

when I see your face on a t-shirt

I just pray to god it's hard wishing it would get

better/And watch it, cause death or funerals bring our

family together/Now look, we done lost a brother, your

son done lost a father

Life ain't promised us so tell somebody you love

them/You'll never know when they'll be here tomorrow...

I drove through the city listening to Master P's *Goodbye To My Homies*; I swear this shit ain't feel right. Saying RIP in front of Jah's name sounded spooky as fuck, but this was my reality and as hard as it was for me to face it, I knew I had to. I sipped from my bottle and drove around, ultimately ending up at the cemetery.

Climbing out my car, I slowly walked to Jah's grave. The fresh flowers that were planted let me know that somebody had visited previously. I hadn't been since the funeral; I guess the fear of facing the reality kept me from visiting. Today was different though and I just needed to be in his space for a little while.

Taking a seat, I sipped my bottled and stared at the freshly covered grave. A tear slipped out of my eye and I quickly wiped it away.

"Damn Jah man, why it had to be you, lil bruh? I would give anything to switch places with you, just so you can be here to see your seed come into this world. Megan shut us all out, but I still go check on her and shit; she just can't deal man, none of us can. Shit has been fucked up for me man; I can't even wrap my mind around the fact that I'll never see you again. Fuck Jah, this shit is hard man! You was my lil brother, my right hand, and one of the only people I trusted; now you gone over some fuck ass shit. Don't worry though little brother, them niggas gon get what's coming to them and that's on life."

I talked and drank for the next couple of hours, the sun was starting to set, so I decided to leave. Standing to my feet, I stumbled slightly before quickly gaining my footing. Looking up in the sky, the wind blew extra hard for a few seconds and I knew that was Jah's way of telling me that he was with me.

Chuckling slightly, I nodded my head and walked back to my car. A figure leaning against my car slowed my stride; the closer I got, I realized it was Zena.

"What's up Z? What you doing here?"

"I was driving by and I saw your truck, how you doing?" she asked sincerely.

"It's a process," I told her.

"About what happened earlier-"

"Don't worry about it, we good." I shrugged.

I knew I should've stopped her when she walked closer to me, but the Hennessey in my system and that fact that she was looking good as fuck caused me to let her wrap her arms around my waist. Softly kissing my lips, my hands found her ass and it was on from there as we hungrily kissed each other.

"You wanna follow me home?" she asked with lust in her eyes.

Now, the smart thing to do would've been to say no, but I needed somebody and she was there, so I said fuck it.

"Yea, I'll follow you," I told her.

She smiled and I could've sworn I hear her ass say, "I knew you would come back, you always do." But, I couldn't be too sure.

I shrugged it off and hopped into my truck. Something told me that I was making the biggest mistake of my life, but right now, I really didn't give a fuck. Azuri flashed across my brain, then I remembered our argument from earlier and pushed her to the back. As if that wasn't bad enough, she called. I stared at the phone and let it roll over to voicemail before turning the phone off completely. At this point, I just didn't give a fuck about much and I'm sure that it was the Hennessey talking.

Fucking with Zena was sure to get me into a world of trouble, but I would cross that bridge when I got to it.

Chapter 32: Azuri

The whole time I was at work I was constantly calling Kashmir's phone. I felt like he took everything I said out of context. I wanted to explain things to him so he would have a better understanding. The fact he wasn't answering my calls pissed me off but when he turned off his phone I felt as though I was on ten.

As soon as the shift manager came into the store I was gone with the quickness. I jumped in the car and went straight to the house hoping he was there. When I pulled up his car was no where in sight. I parked the car and ran into the house only to find it empty. Feeling as if I just made the biggest mistake of my life I laid across the bed.

I began second guessing my decision to turn down his proposal. Just because he proposed didn't mean we had to get married right away right?

"Fuck!" I screamed out loud in frustration. I tried calling his phone once again and just like before it went straight to voicemail.

Since I didn't have anything else to do I decided it would be best to cook dinner like I was going to do before the proposal. As I was walking toward the bedroom door, I noticed Kashmir's IPad sitting on the dresser. I quickly picked it up and went to the find my IPhone app. I typed in the necessary information and in a matter of seconds I had Kashy's location.

The address wasn't familiar to me which immediately had me on alert. Walking into my closet I traded in my work clothes for a pair of basket ball shorts, a black tee and some jays. Kashmir has been teaching me how to use a gun but I wasn't all the way comfortable with that. Instead I decided to take the bat Kashy kept in his closet. I snatched up the Ipad leaving my phone on the dresser and I was out the door.

I drove to the address with a million and one things going through my mind. None of the thoughts were good ones, they went from him cheating on me to him having a whole secret family. The more I thought about the issue the worse the situation became in my head.

Pulling up to the address I saw Kashmir's car and another car parked out front. I was glad that the person didn't live in an apartment building because if they did I would've had to knock on all the doors.

I decided to leave the bat in the car until I found out what the situation was. I didn't want to pop up at a friends or families house acting all crazy and shit. I knocked on the door a couple of times before I heard someone yelling on the other side.

"Who the fuck is knocking on my door when I'm trying to get some." The voice belonged to a female but I wasn't going to overreact just yet. The door swung open and the last person I expected to answer the door was standing there with a smug look on her face.

"The fuck are you doing at my door hoe?" Zena asked.

I nodded my head saying nothing as I walked away from her front door. Zena was yelling and talking shit while I made my way to my car. I unlocked the back door and pulled out the bat ready for war.

"Bitch you better get the fuck away from my house with that shit! I will call the cops on yo crazy ass." Zena spat.

I smirked at her then went over to Kashmir's car and busted out both tail lights.

"Tell that nigga to get the fuck out here now!" I spat.

"I'm not telling nobody shit but the cops." She yelled back.

"You think I'm playing with you?" I busted out the windows in Kashmir's car then went over to what I assumed to be Zena's cars and started doing the same.

"Zena the fuck takin' yo ass so long." I heard Kashmir say.

The sound of his voice irked the shit out of me at this moment. He came to the door and his eyes automatically landed on me.

"Zuri the fuck yo silly lil ass doing out here fuckin' up my car and shit."

"Gotti you have no right to fucking question me. This is the type of shit we doing? When you don't get your way you run to this bitch. You a grown ass fucking man doing childish shit."

"He comes running back because he knows I'm the only bitch that can handle him."

"You a real delusional bitch you know that. You can't handle Gotti he came back to you because he knows he can walk all over you. You have no back bone nor do you stand up for yourself. When he ask you to jump yo dumb ass says how high. The nigga tells you to swallow you're on your knees faster than a fucking speeding bullet."

"I don't know who you think you.."

"Zena shut the fuck up." Kashmir gritted mushing her back in the house. He closed the door starring at me with death in his eyes.

"The fuck you doing here Azuri?" he asked.

"No what are you doing here Gotti? You really that mad because I told you I won't marry you right now. I said RIGHT NOW isn't the right time. You actin' like I told yo ass never." I wanted to inch closer to him with the bat but I knew better.

"You just don't fucking get it do you Azuri. You got a nigga feeling things he never felt before. I'm so fucking scared of losing you that I'm willing to marry yo annoying ass. But instead of you seeing the good in the situation all you see is me doing it because I lost my brother. Yeah I lost my brother and that put shit in perspective for me but it doesn't take away from my feelings for you."

"Instead of you talking about it with me, you went and ran to this bitch. Gotti like really."

He rubbed his hand down his face as if he was looking for the right words to say. If you asked me nothing he said could fix what was taking place right now. We have had arguments before and not once has he ran to another bitch so what made this so fucking different.

"Azuri just go home and I'll see you when I get there." He sighed.

"Nigga you must be stupid if you think I will be at home waiting for you to finish your little fuck."

"Why the fuck don't you listen man that's yo fucking..."

In the middle of Kashmir's sentence a black truck pulled up. Kashmir and I both looked on trying to see who the person inside was.

"Damn Gotti you got Stink out here showing her ass behind you. Nigga you know that's rule number three in this game." Tamir smirked coming and standing next to me. Instead of inching away like I knew I should've my ass stayed right there.

"Azuri get the fuck over here now!" Gotti gritted moving off of the porch.

"Don't let that nigga talk to you like that Stink. His ungrateful ass don't deserve you."

"And what are you trying to say that you do." I smirked.

"You would have to take that chance and find out." He smiled.

"Y'all really about to do this like I'm not fucking standing here?" Gotti laughed. He pulled two guns out from his waist band and pointed one at me and one at Tamir.

"The police should be on their way so I suggest you get the fuck away from my house bitch!" Zena yelled finally coming back outside.

"Zena since when did you become a cop caller?" Tamir laughed.

"Tamir wha...wha...what are you doing here" Zena stuttered.

"Oh you really thought I wasn't going to come back and handle you the same way you handled my baby." He laughed. The sound of two more guns cocking replaced the sound of laughter.

"I don't have time for this shit." The tension between these two was thick as fuck and I didn't want any parts.

I went to walk away but Gotti's next words stopped me in my tracks.

"Azuri you're not going any fucking where. Till death do us part remember." His voice was cold, it sent an eery chill down my spine that I couldn't ignore.

"I never said I do."

"You just did." Where the last words I remember before the chaos began.

To Be Continued...

Made in the USA
Lexington, KY
02 February 2018